Omar turned. Inches separated them.

The seconds ticked by, neither of them moving, their gazes locked. And then Karine went to her toes.

His mouth touched hers. Her fingers skimmed down his arms in a touch so light he could barely feel it, which made it all the more exciting somehow.

He kept the kiss light, exploring her mouth.

Karine stepped back all too soon. Her eyes shone with surprise, desire and uncertainty.

He knew her well enough to know she'd need time to process the line they'd just crossed, so he took two steps backward, giving her space.

His gaze hooked on something over Karine's shoulder. A flash of metal. "Get down!"

He grabbed Karine on instinct. They hit the ground hard enough to rattle his jaw.

The gunshot reverberated in the air around them.

LAKESIDE SECRETS

K.D. RICHARDS

INTRIGUE

Recycling programs for this product may not exist in your area.

ISBN-13: 978-1-335-45681-6

Lakeside Secrets

This is a work of fiction. Names, characters, places and incidents are either the product of the author's imagination or are used fictitiously. Any resemblance to actual persons, living or dead, businesses, companies, events or locales is entirely coincidental.

For questions and comments about the quality of this book, please contact us at CustomerService@Harlequin.com.

TM and ® are trademarks of Harlequin Enterprises ULC.

Harlequin Enterprises ULC
22 Adelaide St. West, 41st Floor
Toronto, Ontario M5H 4E3, Canada
www.Harlequin.com

MIX
Paper | Supporting responsible forestry
FSC® C021394
www.fsc.org

Printed in Lithuania

K.D. Richards is a native of the Washington, DC, area, who now lives outside Toronto with her husband and two sons. You can find her at kdrichardsbooks.com.

Books by K.D. Richards

Harlequin Intrigue

West Investigations

Pursuit of the Truth
Missing at Christmas
Christmas Data Breach
Shielding Her Son
Dark Water Disappearance
Catching the Carling Lake Killer
Under the Cover of Darkness
A Stalker's Prey
Silenced Witness
Lakeside Secrets

Visit the Author Profile page at Harlequin.com.

CAST OF CHARACTERS

***Karine Eloi*—**Marilee Eloi's daughter, who is on a misson to bring her mother's killer to justice.

***Ranger Omar Monroe*—**Karine's best friend and a Carling Lake ranger.

***Marilee Eloi*—**Karine's mother and Jean's former wife.

***Jean Eloi*—**Karine's father and the prime suspect in his former wife's unsolved murder.

***Deputy Shep Coben*—**Deputy in charge of current and cold cases.

***James West*—**Omar's friend and part-time West Investigations employee who helps Omar and Karine investigate.

Prologue

There's no need to panic. Karine Eloi will probably stay in Carling Lake just long enough to put the house up for sale then she'll return to that godforsaken city where she lives. After all, she's some kind of big-shot financial person in Los Angeles. Nobody would trade that life for Carling Lake.

Marilee Eloi's killer just had to keep a clear head.

The killer had been lucky, damned lucky, for more than twenty years. No one had even thought to connect them to Marilee's murder. Besides, folks in this town wanted to believe Marilee had died at the hands of an outsider, that one of their own couldn't have done something so evil. And they'd had the perfect scapegoat. Jean Eloi. Even his name was snooty.

Jean had snuck right in and married a hometown girl and the Carling Lakers hadn't liked that one bit. It hadn't taken more than a few well-placed rumors, the best kind if you asked the killer, to get people casting suspicious glances and talking all about how Marilee's highfalutin husband must have been the murderer.

If the killer had known she'd been in the house with her mother, little Karine might have fallen prey to the big bad burglar that night too. Why leave a witness when you didn't have to? Karine wasn't a witness, though. She'd slept through the whole thing and that was what had saved her life all these years.

But now she was back in town and that was bound to kick up memories that the killer would rather stay buried. That new sheriff was far too progressive for the killer's liking. What if he decided to show off by delving into a more than twenty-year-old murder?

One problem at a time. The killer would have to keep a close watch on Marilee's girl. Maybe give her a reason not to linger in Carling Lake. And if there was any cause to worry…well then, the killer would just have to finish the job that was started twenty-three years ago.

Chapter One

It was far too quiet in Carling Lake, New York. That was the problem, Karine Eloi thought as she turned onto her back and stared up at the ceiling, willing sleep to come. She was used to the sounds of Los Angeles. The ever-present car horns, shouts, music and other assorted fracas of the city. The high-pitched squealing and fervent scratching coming from the attic above her was one thing that did remind her of Los Angeles. Or rather, the dump of an apartment she'd lived in when she'd first moved to the city. She made a mental note to put mousetraps on her shopping list and tried to tune out the sounds.

When she'd arrived in Carling Lake earlier that evening, she'd stood on the sidewalk in front of the house, looking at the place that had been her home for the first twelve years of her life. It looked familiar, but time and tragedy had dulled her memories of the place. But while the town and house she lived in had faded in her mind, the boy who'd lived next door never had. Omar Monroe had been her best friend since they were five years old. Even after her father had moved them three hours away to Springtree, Connecticut, she and Omar had remained close. Not even her move across the country to Los Angeles for college, and her subsequent decision to stay on the west coast, could break the bonds of their friendship.

Karine had hoped to see him when she reached town, but traffic had put her behind schedule and the house next door to the one she now owned, the house Omar had lived in his entire life, was dark by the time she'd arrived. She knew that as the only full-time state park ranger assigned to the Carling Lake area, Omar often had to work late, but she was excited and more than a little anxious to see him; it had been six months since he'd come out to visit her in Los Angeles. She remembered the punch in the gut she'd felt when she dropped him off at the airport, how difficult it had been to watch him walk away, knowing she wouldn't see him the next day.

She turned onto her side and closed her eyes. She was sure she'd see Omar soon enough. Right now, she had to get some sleep. But her mind wouldn't shut off. Coming back to her childhood home had opened up a Pandora's box of emotions that wouldn't be quelled by slumber.

The two-story home was an imposing mix of brick and clapboard. But it had been well maintained, just as Mr. Hill, the lawyer who had managed the family trust, had told her. The home had been in Karine's family for nearly sixty years, built by her grandfather, Wayne Barstol, who'd had the forethought to pass it to his daughter, Marilee, and then on to her, his granddaughter, via a trust so that it would remain in the family. After her grandfather had passed away, Karine and her parents had moved in. She may have been young when she'd lived here, but she remembered how much her mother had loved the house and Carling Lake.

A memory floated to the forefront of her mind as she'd

stood on the sidewalk, peering up at her childhood home. Her, her mother and her father sitting on a swing hung from the porch ceiling, cuddled under a blanket on a starry night. And laughter. Lots of laughter.

There'd always been a lot of laughter when her mom was alive. Not after though.

Karine couldn't remember what her father's laugh sounded like or the last time she'd seen him smile.

She swallowed the tears that rose in her throat. Her father hadn't wanted her to ever return to Carling Lake. After her mother's death—her murder—twenty-three years earlier and the suspicion that had swirled around him, Jean Eloi had packed their bags and moved them to Connecticut, never looking back. He'd wanted Karine to do the same.

Never look back.

But Karine couldn't just plow ahead like her father had. She'd been there. She'd seen…something. Her dreams, her nightmares really, made that quite clear. But what had she seen?

Her dreams had never been clear enough to answer that question. For her father, it was tough enough dealing with the reality that his beloved Marilee was gone. The who and the why wouldn't bring her back, so he'd pressed on, remarried and gotten on with his life.

For her, it was the opposite. Each year, each moment lately, the need within her to know who and why grew stronger. Why had her mother been taken from her? Who had shattered her childhood and changed her life so irrevocably? Two months ago, she'd turned thirty-five and, by the terms of the trust left by her grandfather, become the outright owner of the family home. She'd known what she had to do. Go to Carling Lake and get justice for her mother.

She'd made it to Carling Lake. Now what?

She was a financial analyst without the first idea of where to start investigating a murder.

Her mind churned through what she knew about her mother's murder. Twenty-three years ago, while Karine had slept upstairs and her father was at a faculty function, someone had broken into the house. The then sheriff had theorized it was a burglar who hadn't realized anyone was at home. Her mother must have awakened and confronted the intruder. The confrontation had ended with her mother being bludgeoned.

There was so much about that night and the days after that was foggy for Karine, but she remembered talking to a policeman with bushy gray eyebrows and kind eyes. Telling him she hadn't heard or seen anything after her mother had put her to bed for the night. She remembered, too, hearing the police officer speaking to another cop.

I don't think she saw anything. Small blessing.

For more than twenty years, she'd also believed that, but now she wasn't so sure anymore. As her thirty-fifth birthday approached, the dreams had begun. Vivid dreams. Her mother lying on the floor in the hallway. A red river around her. And a figure over her mother's body.

In the dream, the figure was never clear enough to tell who it was or even if it was a man or a woman. At first, she'd thought it was nothing more than a dream, but each time she had it, the details became clearer, sharper. The fireplace poker was on the floor next to her mother. The red river, she realized, was blood encircling her mother's head. The back door to the house was standing open. She could see it all as if she was there. Or had been there. Everything except the face of the person who'd killed her mother.

Karine had all but given up on the police ever naming a suspect, much less convicting anyone, until a few weeks ago. That was when she'd received an email from Amber Burke Spindler, one of her mother's closest friends.

She remembered Amber from when she was younger, even though Amber had made no attempt to reach out to Karine after she and her father had moved to Connecticut. No one from Carling Lake had made any effort to keep up with her or her father, except Omar and his parents.

She gave up on sleep and reached for her phone on the nightstand. She scrolled to the opened email chain from Amber.

Karine,
You may not remember me. My name is Amber Burke Spindler, and I was friends with your mother. Good friends at one point. There is something I need to speak to you about. It's important. About your mother. It's too much to type out and too dangerous to put on paper. I need to tell you in person. Please get back to me. And tell no one.
Amber Burke Spindler

She'd thought about the email for weeks before she'd finally responded. Her father had never liked talking about her mother or the way her mother had died. Whenever she'd attempted to bring it up, he always said it was a tragedy and that she should try not to think about it. But the older she'd gotten, the less she'd heeded his advice. She'd searched the *Carling Lake Weekly* online for news on the murder and, talking to Amber, someone who'd known her mother and been around during the time of her murder, just might get her the answers she needed. Karine knew the police theory was that her mother had surprised a burglar. But something about that explanation just seemed off.

She hadn't told anyone about the email from Amber. Not even her best friend and Carling Lake resident, Omar Monroe. She knew he'd have pressed her to tell the authorities about Amber having reached out to her, and she didn't want to do that until she knew what Amber had to say. She'd tried to convince Amber to disclose whatever it was she wanted to tell her via email and had even offered to call or video chat, but Amber hadn't budged.

In the end, curiosity had won out. She'd used some of the vacation time she had banked from years of early mornings and late nights at her investment firm and headed to Carling Lake. She hadn't told Omar about Amber's email, but he was aware that she hoped to convince the sheriff to reinvigorate the investigation into her mother's murder. She'd also known her father would try to talk her out of it if he realized the truth, so she'd told him only that she was coming to Carling Lake to ready the house for sale.

She'd arranged to meet Amber the next afternoon at Amber's house in an upper-class section of Carling Lake where lots of the rich part-time residents lived. Amber could afford to live there having married then divorced Daton Spindler, heir to Spindler Plastics.

Karine was anxious to hear what Amber knew about her mother's death that was so important she couldn't tell her in an email or video chat and why, if it was so important, she hadn't told the police.

She set the phone aside, swung her feet over the side of the bed, and rose. She was too wired to sleep. What she needed was a cup of chamomile tea to help settle her nerves. Luckily, she'd arrived in town with just enough time to drop off her suitcases and head to the supermarket before it closed since 24/7 shopping hadn't seemed to have made its way to Carling Lake just yet.

She padded down the stairs; the moon providing more than enough light to guide her. In the kitchen, she hit the switch for the penlight that hung over the stove, but left the brighter recessed lighting off. She'd found an old-fashioned stainless-steel kettle in the cabinet next to the sink earlier that evening and filled it now. While the water in the kettle heated, she stepped over to the sliding-glass doors that led from the kitchen to the back porch and slid them open.

Mr. Hill had rented out the house over the years and it had been several months since the last renter had vacated. She'd left the windows open for several hours after dinner, yet the air inside the house was still stale and heavy.

Karine turned back to the floor-to-ceiling pantry and reached inside for the thin can that held her favorite brand of chamomile tea leaves.

A muscular arm clamped around her waist, yanking her backward. The can clattered to the tile floor, spilling tea leaves at her feet. The scream that ripped from her throat was cut off by a gloved hand.

OMAR MONROE DIDN'T know how anyone could choose to live in a place where they couldn't see the stars. He'd bought his childhood home from his parents when they'd decided to move to Florida and now he looked up at the dark blue sky rimmed with purple and dotted with twinkling stars. It was breathtaking. He glanced over at the house next door. He had hoped to be home by the time his best friend, Karine Eloi, landed in town, but when he'd arrived, the lights inside the house next door had been out. He knew Karine had arrived, though, by the rented sedan parked in the usually empty driveway.

As a state park ranger, he spent the day just how he liked to spend every day: protecting and preserving the Carling Lake Forest. He'd lost track of time when he'd been out on patrol today. It wasn't like him, but since he'd earlier discovered several dead birds along a stream and creek feeding into Carling Lake, he'd been taking even more care on his patrols, on the lookout for any abnormalities or animals that appeared to be in distress. He'd noted some concerning issues, enough so that he'd been authorized to conduct water samplings of the stream and creek, looking for pollutants. But those samples had come back clean and, as far as his boss was concerned, that had been the end of it.

But that wasn't the end of it. Not for him. He knew this forest as well as he knew himself. He'd grown up in Carling Lake, playing in these woods, fishing, camping and hiking with his father. He'd known from a young age that he wanted to become a state ranger. Protecting this particular forest was a job he took seriously, and he'd been overjoyed when the position had opened up four years earlier and he'd been able to transfer from his then position in Buffalo, New York, to his hometown of Carling Lake.

But something was off inside his forest. The town's economy depended on tourism, but some of Carling Lake's visitors didn't realize how delicate the forest's ecosystem was. Any introduction of outside contaminants, even accidentally, could throw that system out of balance. And if it wasn't an accident? Ecoterrorism was more prevalent than a lot of people realized. Without knowing what he was dealing with, Omar couldn't pinpoint a motive or know what corrective steps might have to be taken. He needed to figure out what was going on, and fast. Before irreversible damage was done.

He glanced again at the house next door, determined to make time to spend with his best friend while she was in town. As much time as he could finagle.

He let out a frustrated sigh. It had been six months since he'd last seen Karine. Waiting one more day wouldn't kill him.

A little ping of awareness in the center of his chest argued the opposite. That ping had been happening more and more frequently. Whenever he talked to or texted with Karine. Whenever he thought about her, which was, he was willing to admit to himself, more and more often. He loved being a park ranger, but it was a solitary profession. He spent a great deal of time in his truck or out patrolling through the forest. Plenty of time for a man to think, and lately the only thing he could think about was Karine.

Karine, his friend, he reminded himself not for the first time. It was only natural that, lately, his mind had turned to her more. She'd turned thirty-five and announced she was coming back to Carling Lake for the first time in twenty-three years to take up her own investigation into her mother's murder. As happy as he was to have his best friend next door instead of three thousand miles away, he was worried about her desire to delve into her mother's death.

Omar didn't pretend to understand what she must feel, having been in the house when her mother was murdered, but he knew she'd struggled with nightmares over the years. Marilee Eloi's homicide hadn't been solved, and although it was technically still an open case, there had been no new leads in nearly two decades. He wasn't sure what Karine hoped to find, but he hoped it wasn't trouble. No matter what, though, he planned to be by her side through it all.

He took a deep breath of crisp, clean mountain air and tried to settle. The night was quiet, like most nights in Carling Lake. Just how he liked it. Every so often, he'd hear a small animal scuttle across the undersized yard that separated the back porch of his house from the forest beyond.

He swallowed a sigh, burrowing deeper into his lounge chair and taking a long sip from the half-empty beer bottle in his hand.

Relax. You'll see Karine in a few hours.

His phone buzzed and he knew without looking who it was. Only a few other people in town worked crazy hours similar to his, although his friend was supposed to be packing for his vacation in Maui, which was to start the next day.

Karine has arrived?

Sheriff Lance Webb was his closest friend in town and he'd heard all about Karine, although the two had never met. Unfortunately, Lance and his girlfriend, Simone, were going to be on a long-awaited vacation for most of Karine's visit.

Shouldn't you be packing for your trip?

I'm multitasking. And don't change the subject.

Lance hadn't said anything explicitly, but Omar suspected he had picked up on his growing feelings for Karine. Ever since Lance had coupled up with Simone, he'd been pushing Omar to find a nice woman and settle down. The idea wasn't unappealing, but there was only one woman who came to mind wherever Omar thought about making a commitment.

Karine has arrived. I had to work late so I haven't had a chance to welcome her home yet.

Join you for a nightcap?

How sweet of you, but I'm exhausted.

Not me! Her. Ask her to join you for a nightcap.

I think she's already gone to bed. The lights in the house were off when I got home.

The sound of something crashing jolted him from the text conversation with Lance.

A scream, loud and terrified, had him on his feet, tucking his phone into his pocket as he did, jumping over the porch railing and darting for Karine's house in an instant.

It only took seconds to assess the scene in front of him. A masked man. A terrified Karine clawing at the arm around her neck.

"Let her go," Omar growled, stepping through the open sliding-glass door.

Karine's eyes widened, fear radiating from them.

The masked man's eyes narrowed. He locked his arm

tighter around Karine's neck, drawing a pained squeak from her.

It was only the possibility that Karine could get hurt in the scrum that kept Omar from launching himself at the intruder.

He'd rushed over without stopping to grab his gun, but no matter, he was well versed in hand-to-hand combat. There was no doubt in his mind that he could overpower the intruder, who was only about five-eleven and thin, maybe a hundred and thirty pounds. He just needed to get Karine out of harm's way first.

"Let her go," he repeated.

"You want me to let her go?" the man said in a voice that sounded as if he was trying to disguise it. "Fine."

The masked man gave Karine a hard shove, propelling her forward unsteadily.

Omar caught her before she fell headfirst into the countertop. The intruder darted from the kitchen and back toward the living room and front door.

He steadied Karine, studying her for injuries. Even in bare feet and pajamas, she was statuesque. Her long, light brown hair was disheveled from the attack and her toffee-colored cheeks were pink with fear and exertion. "Are you okay?"

"Yeah. Yes," she said, shaken, but with no obvious injuries that he could see.

"Okay. Stay here," Omar ordered before taking off after the man.

The front door was open. He ran outside onto the porch, looking up and down the street, but saw no one. Whoever had broken in was gone, lost in the shadows.

Omar walked back into the house, locking the front door, then doing the same for the rear sliding-glass doors leading from the porch to the kitchen.

"Are you sure you're okay?" he asked, joining Karine on the sofa, pulling her in close. She wasn't the only one shaken by the intrusion and he needed to feel her warmth to assure himself she hadn't been hurt.

He pulled away enough to look down on her while still keeping his arms around her. "Not much of a welcome to town, is it?"

She gave him a tight smile. "So far, I'm not impressed." She pulled out of his arms. "How did you—"

"I was out on my back porch, having a beer and unwinding from the day, when I heard you scream."

"Thank goodness you did. Who was that guy? I guess the house has probably attracted a lot of vagrants sitting here vacant like it's been for the last couple of months."

"Actually, I have been keeping an eye on it for you. I didn't get a good look at whoever attacked you, but no one's been hanging around here. At least, not that I've seen."

"Oh, well..."

"We need to call the sheriff's office and file a report."

"Oh, I don't think all that is necessary. It's late and—"

"It's definitely necessary." Omar pulled his phone from his pocket. "You might want to take a look around and see if anything is missing while we wait."

"I wouldn't even know if there was anything missing. The trustee rented out the house as a furnished rental, and while everything here is technically mine, none of this is really mine. Everything I brought with me is upstairs in the master bedroom."

It was just as well. He didn't want her leaving his side, and he didn't think whoever had broken in had done so to rob the place. The house had sat empty for the last several months, giving any burglar the perfect opportunity to ransack the place well before Karine's arrival.

He reported the attempted burglary and was told a car would be sent right out, then he called Lance and conveyed what had happened.

"This was not exactly the way I imagined my homecoming."

"I'm just glad you're here." Omar put an arm around Karine's shoulder and pulled her to him. "And that I was close by."

And that was exactly where he planned to be until he was sure she was safe in Carling Lake.

Chapter Two

When the doorbell rang a short time later, Omar went to answer it. Karine had never been so relieved to see her best friend. She wasn't sure what would have happened had he not bounded through the sliding doors. She was no shrinking violet, but the intruder had caught her off guard.

A pinch that was more attraction than relief hit her. She watched him stride into the room. His six-foot frame packed all the muscle one would expect of a man whose job included frequent hikes through the woods and daily physical activities. But it wasn't just Omar's physical attributes that turned heads. He had a presence, a warmth and intelligence that he exuded wherever he went. It was a charm that naturally drew people to him.

Omar led a uniformed sheriff's deputy into the living room where she sat.

The deputy took off his hat as he entered the house, revealing blond hair that was rapidly going gray and thinning, but his dark brown eyes were shrewd. He was in his late forties, with a round midsection that hung over his waistband quite a bit.

"Mr. Monroe," the deputy said, earning a nod from Omar before he turned to Karine. "Ma'am, I'm Deputy Shep Coben. I don't believe I've had the pleasure."

"Karine Eloi," she said, pushing to her feet and offering her hand.

Deputy Coben studied Karine through narrow eyes. "Eloi? Any relation to Jean Eloi?"

"He's my father." She gave the deputy's hand a quick shake before dropping it.

"Then you must be Marilee Barstol's girl."

"Marilee Barstol Eloi was my mother, yes."

"Huh." Deputy Coben sniffed, his gaze traveling over the room. "Guess it makes sense to find you in the Barstol house. That's what we natives call this place."

She bristled at the way the deputy's eyes swept over her and the house as if they were specimens for him to inspect and dissect. He struck her as a man who did that a lot. Inspected and dissected, looking for a person's weaknesses and ways to exploit those weaknesses.

"Technically, it's the Eloi place now," Karine said sharply.

Shep smiled without warmth. "It'll always be the Barstol place to native Carling Lakers, ma'am. I was new to the department when your mother died, but Marilee, rest her soul, and her daddy, Wayne, your grandpa, were part of our community."

The space between them weighed heavily with the implication that Karine and her father, Jean Eloi, were not a part of the Carling Lake community.

Jean Eloi had always been resistant to talking about his late wife and the years the family had lived in this town. Whenever Karine had asked about her mother or the break-in that had led to her death, her father would become visibly upset and change the subject as quickly as he could. She knew he had terrible memories of this place, not only because of her mother's murder, but also because he was a suspect.

Her father had been a struggling new professor working at the nearby community college when he'd met Marilee, the town sweetheart. Karine had gotten her father to open up enough that she knew he and her mother had met at a workshop on conservation at the community college and they'd fallen for each other hard. "Love at first sight" was how her father had described it. They'd married three months after meeting, much to the chagrin of Grandfather Wayne and many others in town. Eleven months later, Karine was born, which had done little to soften her grandfather's dislike of her father. It was commonly rumored around town that Jean had only married Marilee for the home and extensive land holdings she was set to inherit when her father passed away. It was why her grandfather had set up the trust to ensure that her father would never get his hands on any of Marilee or Karine's inheritance. Even though he'd technically inherited very little because of the trust, there had still been whispers that he'd killed his wife for her money.

"Why don't you tell me what happened here tonight?" Deputy Coben pulled a small notebook from the pocket of his coat, along with a stub pencil, and turned to a clean page. "Who wants to go first?" His gaze danced between Karine and Omar.

Omar made a gesture in her direction, indicating she should go first. She recounted the night's events, from being unable to sleep and rising to make tea, to seeing Omar bound through the sliding-glass door.

Shep turned to Omar with suspicion in his eyes. "That's

mighty convenient, Omar. How did you know this young woman was in need of assistance?"

Waves of irritation flowed from Omar, but he kept his tone polite. "You know, I live next door and Karine and I have been friends since we were children. I was just home from my shift and having a beer on my back porch when I heard a scream. I figured I should check it out."

Shep scowled. "You know you're nothing but a civilian within the town limits of Carling Lake. Your jurisdiction is limited to the trees," he said condescendingly.

"I know where my jurisdiction ends, Shep," Omar responded, his tone sharpening. "But Karine is my friend. If she needs me, I'll be there, jurisdiction or not."

"And I, for one, count that as a good thing." A tall Black man in a sheriff's uniform strode through the front door that Shep had left open when he'd been let into the house. "I think we all ought to be thankful Omar was nearby. This could have ended much differently if he hadn't been."

Shep shrank back with a pronounced grimace on his face as the man joined them in the living room.

Karine shivered. She thought again about what could have happened if he hadn't been close by. What had happened in this very house years earlier?

Omar must have sensed the direction of her thoughts. He wrapped his arm around her and pulled her in close. She inhaled his piney scent and sank into his arms.

The man held out a hand to Karine. "Sheriff Lance Webb."

"Karine Eloi," she said, giving Lance's hand a firmer shake than she'd afforded the deputy.

"I've heard so much about you from Omar. Once you're

settled, we'll have to have coffee and you can tell me all of his secrets," he teased.

The sheriff smiled, and she relaxed a touch more, which she suspected had been the sheriff's intention.

Sheriff Webb turned to Omar. "Omar."

"Lance. Thanks for coming." The men shook hands.

"Sheriff, I was just finishing up taking these witness's statements," Shep interjected.

Lance turned to his deputy. "Good. Why don't you go canvass the neighbors and see if anyone is awake? Maybe someone saw something."

Shep's mouth turned down into a frown, but he closed his notebook and pushed it back into his pocket. "Yes, sir."

Deputy Coben turned on his heel and left through the door the sheriff had entered.

Omar's brow rose. "You've got a problem with that one."

Lance swiped his hat from his head and wiped his brow. "I know. It's been brewing since I was voted in as sheriff over him. I'll have to deal with it at some point, but not today. Right now, I want to make sure you are both okay."

"I'm fine," Karine said.

"I'm good. The guy ran off almost as soon as I came through the door," Omar added.

Karine chewed her bottom lip. "Omar doesn't think this was a robbery attempt. Do you?"

The sheriff shared a look with Omar, but neither answered her, which she guessed was an answer of a sort.

"Miss Eloi—" Lance started.

"Karine, please."

"Karine," he began again with a tight smile. "I'd like to gather all the facts before I make any determinations."

"That's very diplomatic, Sheriff. I take it you know about my mother's murder in this house twenty-three years ago?"

He nodded. "I'm familiar with the circumstances. It remains an open case with the sheriff's department."

"Omar doesn't want to scare me, but I know him too well. He's concerned my burglar wasn't a burglar at all. That whoever broke in here was targeting me and that it might have to do with my mother's death."

Lance glanced at Omar.

"I didn't say that," Omar said quickly.

Karine rolled her eyes. "You didn't have to. I've known you since we were five. You don't think I know what you're thinking?"

"Karine, I'm sure it's difficult to not have answers to your mother's murder..."

She pushed her shoulders back, stepping away from Omar. "It's not just difficult, Sheriff. It's excruciating. It's been years and still no one has been held to answer. Well, I just officially inherited the house, and I plan to find out why my mother was murdered."

She took a deep breath then and let it out slowly. "Twenty-three years ago my mother was killed in this house. Her murder was never solved. I've come back to Carling Lake to find answers. And to finally get justice for my mother."

OMAR WAS NOT what anyone would call a morning person and getting up at six thirty was not his idea of a good time. Especially not when he'd spent the night before tossing and turning, worried about Karine. He'd wanted to stay over at her place, but she'd declined his offer. Usually, he admired her fearless independence, but not when someone might be targeting her. Since it had been late, Lance had suggested they all get some rest and meet for an early breakfast before he headed to the airport to begin his vacation. Thus, his early-morning wake-up call.

He had hoped to catch Karine that morning so they could head over to Rosie's diner together, but he'd hit the snooze button one too many times, it seemed. By the time he made it out of his house, Karine's car was already gone from her driveway.

He ignored the anxiety that bubbled in his chest as he drove to Rosie's. Carling Lake was generally a safe town, although it had seen its fair share of crime recently. But no one would attempt to harm Karine in broad daylight.

He was sure she was perfectly safe. Still, his anxiety didn't abate until he pulled the door to the diner open and stepped inside. He scanned the L-shaped space, his eyes falling on Karine almost as if pulled by an unseen force. She looked across the room, meeting his gaze and sending his heart into a gallop. Dark circles rimmed her light brown eyes, telling the story of how her night had gone after he, Lance and Deputy Coben had left her. But she was still beautiful.

He slid into the chair next to her at the table.

"About time, Monroe," she said, bumping his shoulder playfully. She knew about his aversion to early mornings.

"I'd planned to catch you so we could head here together, but I couldn't stop hitting the snooze button."

She laughed, and something in him lightened. "Between the jet lag and the adrenaline, I couldn't go back to sleep. I went out for a run, showered and made it here early."

Omar frowned. "You shouldn't have gone running by

yourself. We don't know if last night was a one-off or something more serious."

"I'm not going to hide out, Omar."

Now was as good a time as any to bring up a subject he knew she was going to hate. "Before Lance gets here, I wanted to talk to you."

She held up her hand. "If you're going to try to talk me out of searching for my mother's killer, you can just save it."

"You should leave this to the professionals."

Her forehead creased. "No offense, but the professionals have had twenty-three years and they haven't been successful at finding my mother's killer. I have to ask myself if that's on purpose or merely incompetence."

A waitress arrived to take their orders before Omar could rally a response. He ordered an egg white omelet and Karine ordered the French toast.

As the waitress left to put their order in with the kitchen, the door to the diner opened again, letting in Lance, followed by James West, a newly minted Carling Lake resident.

James West owned an art gallery on Main Street, but despite his career change, he still looked like the marine he'd been four years before moving to Carling Lake. He was a large man, a few inches over six feet tall, and he was muscled, as if he were still keeping himself ready in case he was called up for combat once again. He was an intimidating presence, but he wore a smile when he entered the diner. The two older men sitting closest to the door called out hellos as James and Lance made their way over to the table.

James's eyes scanned the patrons in the diner quickly and efficiently before landing on Omar and Karine.

Lance exchanged greetings with Omar and Karine and took a seat across from them at the table.

"Omar." James nodded hello, sitting next to Lance. "And Miss Eloi, I presume. It's a pleasure to meet you. I'm James West."

In the year or so since James West had made Carling Lake his home, Omar had gotten to know him pretty well. James and Lance were close, and the three of them often got together to watch a ballgame or just hang out. James had seemed like a decent enough guy. He'd have to be for Lance to have befriended him.

"I asked James to join us. I hope you don't mind, Karine," Lance said.

"Lance thought I might be of help to you two," James added.

"Uh, sure," Karine said hesitantly.

The waitress returned with Omar's and Karine's breakfasts and poured coffee for each of the new arrivals. James and Lance declined to order breakfast.

"I'm curious, Mr. West." Karine spoke when the waitress left again. "Why would the sheriff think you could help me?"

"Because he's a West of West Security and Investigations," Omar said.

Karine stared blankly.

"West Security and Investigations is one of the premier private investigations and personal security firms on the east coast," Lance offered.

"We're expanding to the west coast too," James added with a cheeky grin.

Omar rolled his eyes. James was charismatic, he'd give him that.

"I see." Karine bit her bottom lip.

"You won't find better help than West private eyes," Omar conceded.

"Why don't you explain your situation and then we can figure out how to be of service?" James brought his coffee to his lips and sipped.

Karine's gaze bounced between Omar, Lance and James then, seemingly deciding she could trust them, or maybe just that she had nothing to lose, she began to talk.

"When I was twelve, my mother was murdered. The sheriff back then believed the culprit had to be a tourist or one of the seasonal workers in town, but no suspect was ever officially named. I say officially because, even though the sheriff had chalked it up to a home invasion gone wrong, my father became the prime suspect, at least in the minds of a lot of the people in this town. He had an alibi, but that didn't stop the gossip. He was ostracized."

And so was she, Omar recalled. Some of the kids at school had been cruel. Picking on Karine, calling her father a murderer. Someone had even started a rumor that Karine had killed her mother.

"The people in this town pretty much made his life unbearable," Karine continued. "A few months after my mother's murder, Dad found a teaching job at a community college in Connecticut and we moved away. My mother's case went cold."

"You say your father had an alibi?" James questioned.

Karine nodded. "Yes, he was an assistant professor at Pinewood Community College back then."

Pinewood Community College was about forty minutes north of Carling Lake and many of the local youth began their higher education there in order to save money for a four-year university.

"My father taught botany. He still does, actually. He was at a faculty dinner with twelve other professors from his department the night my mother was killed."

"So why was he a suspect?" James questioned.

"Because he was an outsider. The popular theory was that he'd hired someone to kill his wife and make it look like a break-in. Or that he had somehow snuck out of the dinner. Since it was nothing but a rumor, it didn't have to make a lot of sense even though it decimated my father's reputation," Karine added bitterly. "My mother's family, the Barstols, had been in Carling Lake for generations. My grandfather, Wayne, was a prominent citizen and my mother, Marilee, was beloved by all, according to what little my father will tell me. Grandfather Wayne never liked Dad, and that was enough to poison the town against my father even years after Grandfather's death. But there's no way Dad would have been involved, not just because my mother was the love of his life, but also because he would have never put me in harm's way. He knew I was home with Mom."

"I read the investigation file this morning," Lance said. "You were in the house at the time of your mother's murder."

Karine nodded. "Yes. Asleep in my bedroom. At least, that's what I've always thought."

Omar leaned forward, his eyes narrowed on Karine's face. "What do you mean that's what you'd always thought?" This was news to him. He thought Karine had told him everything about that night.

"For the last twenty-three years, I thought I'd slept through my mother's murder, but I've been having these dreams for the last several months. Vivid dreams where my mother is lying on the floor of our house with blood all around her and someone is there, next to her, but I can't make out their face."

Omar shared worried glances with James and Lance. "You think you saw your mother's killer?"

"I do. I think I blocked it out when I was younger, but it's coming back to me now. Maybe because I've finally inherited the house where she died, but whatever the reason, I have to know the truth. If I can identify my mother's killer, the sheriff—" Karine nodded at Lance "—can reopen the case and she can finally get the justice she deserves."

"You realize these memories could put you in real danger?" Lance said.

"It's a good thing a real-life ranger lives next door." James took another sip of his coffee.

Omar frowned. Next door wasn't nearly close enough. If Karine was truly in danger, it was best if she returned to Los Angeles.

Karine straightened in her seat. "I'm grateful that Omar stepped in last night, but I can take care of myself."

Omar growled. "You're planning on going after a murderer who has gotten away with his crime for decades? You need all the help you can get, not the least of which is someone to watch your back."

"And would that someone be you, Omar?" James questioned.

Omar shifted in his seat to look at Karine directly. "I think the safest thing would be for you to go back to Los Angeles. If you remember anything, you can always call Lance."

She shook her head. "No, I'm not running. Not anymore. I can handle myself, like I said. That guy last night caught me off guard, but it won't happen again.

"I don't need anyone to protect me, but I wouldn't mind help identifying my mother's killer." She turned to look at Lance pleadingly. "Sheriff, I'd like to see the police report from the investigation."

Lance was already shaking his head. "Technically, it's still an open case. I can't risk having you compromise it."

Karine threw her hands up. "Compromise what? Correct me if I'm wrong, but you have no leads and no suspects. When was the last time you even thought about the case before last night?"

Lance pursed his lips.

James tilted his head. "It is unorthodox, Lance, but Karine doesn't have any incentive to compromise the case. Quite the opposite. And maybe something in the file will jog a memory. Give you a fresh lead to follow up on."

Lance glared at James.

"I don't think this is a good idea," Omar offered.

Now Karine glared at him. "Well, I do. And I'm going to investigate no matter who likes it or who helps me."

Omar sighed. He knew that tone. He wasn't going to win this argument.

Lance glanced at his watch. "I have to go. The car is coming in twenty minutes to take me and Simone to the airport. She'll kill me if we miss the flight. Look," he said with a sigh, "I can arrange with my deputy to let you look at the file later today."

Omar watched a brilliant smile bloom across Karine's face and felt something else bloom in his chest.

"But," Lance cautioned, "you can't take anything out of the station."

"Absolutely not, Sheriff. You have my word." Karine smiled.

Lance looked like he already regretted his decision, but he rose and, with hurried goodbyes to each of them, left the diner.

"I guess I should get going too. Karine, it was a pleasure meeting you and, please, if I or West Investigations can do anything to help you, don't hesitate to call. Omar has my number or you can feel free to drop by the gallery or the B and B. I'm usually at one place or the other."

"You are really going to do this then." Omar turned to Karine after James left.

She took his hands in hers. "I know you worry about me, but I have to do this."

"You know your mother's killer could still be out there. You could be drawing the attention of a murderer."

"I hope I do," Karine said with a note of ferocity. "I hope I scare whoever killed my mother so much they make a mistake and reveal themselves."

That was the last thing Omar hoped for. A scared killer was a very dangerous killer.

He couldn't let her do this by herself. No matter what she thought, she was putting herself squarely in the line of fire of a murderer. She needed someone to watch her back.

He leaned back in his chair, resigned. "Okay then. Where do we start?"

Chapter Three

Karine and Omar finished breakfast with a frisson of tension running between them. She knew he wasn't thrilled about her plan, he'd made that clear from the moment she'd told him why she was coming to Carling Lake, but something inside her was pushing her to do this now.

The waitress had just cleared away their plates and left the check when Omar's phone buzzed. He pulled it from his pocket and read the screen. "Lance works fast. He says we can meet Deputy Clarke Bridges at the station to review the file whenever you're ready."

Karine wiped her mouth then tossed the napkin on the table, standing. "I'm ready now."

Omar paid for their breakfast and they stepped out of the diner into the cool morning air. It was late September and it seemed that fall was intent on making itself known.

Karine hurried to her car then turned back, calling out to Omar, who'd parked a few spaces away. "I just realized I don't know where the police station is."

"You can follow me. It's not far."

Omar led the way, and he was right. The station was less than a mile from the diner. Sometime, sooner rather than later, she'd have to take a drive around town and reacquaint herself with Carling Lake. It had been dark when she'd pulled into town last evening, but even in the light of day, nothing they passed on the drive from the diner to the station seemed familiar. She followed Omar into the parking lot, anxious to get a look at the investigation file and happy to be able to do so before she met with Amber.

A pang of guilt ran through her at not having told Omar about the email from Amber yet. But Amber had been clear that she shouldn't tell anyone. Karine would tell him everything as soon as she'd spoken to Amber and found out whatever information she'd been hiding for all these years.

Omar parked in the lot in front of a boxy, white, two-story building with a sign in front of it declaring it was the sheriff's station. She found a parking space a couple of feet closer to the building's entrance and waited for Omar to dismount from his shiny black pickup and join her.

They entered the building together. Omar gave their names to the desk clerk and, after several minutes of waiting, a stout man in a deputy's uniform with thinning brown hair pushed through the doors separating the front reception area from where the deputies sat.

"Clarke." Omar shook the deputy's hand.

"Omar, how are you? It's been a while."

"Oh, same old. Busy."

"I see." The deputy's gaze moved to Karine.

"Deputy Clarke Bridges. Karine Eloi."

Deputy Bridges extended his hand to her. "Ms. Eloi. A pleasure."

"Karine, please."

"So..." Deputy Bridges clapped his hands. "You two can follow me. Lance told me that I should let you see the file on Marilee Eloi. I understand she was your mother," he said, looking at Karine.

"Yes."

"I'm sorry for your loss."

"Thank you. It was a long time ago, but I think it's about time her killer was brought to justice."

Deputy Bridges gestured for them to precede him into a small interview room. "Well, certainly everyone here at the sheriff's department would love to see a killer brought to justice. Now, I've got the file here for you." Deputy Bridges patted the top of a thick accordion-style file folder. "You guys can take your time, but of course, nothing can leave this room." The deputy shifted from foot to foot nervously.

"What is it?" Omar said.

"Shep will be in soon. I know Lance gave you the okay to be here, but while he's on vacation, Shep is technically in charge and, well…"

"It would be best if we weren't here when he got here," Omar said astutely.

Deputy Bridget shrugged. "You know Shep."

"I do know Shep," Omar grumbled. "We'll do our best to get out of your hair before the curmudgeonly deputy arrives."

Deputy Bridges grinned. "I sure would appreciate it."

Deputy Bridges left them to it, closing the door behind him.

Karine took the seat at the table in the room, in front of the file. "I'm glad to see all of the Carling Lake deputy sheriff's aren't like Deputy Coben."

"No, Coben is in a league of his own. He thinks Lance's newfangled city ways of policing are ruining Carling Lake."

"Ah…"

"We've had a bit of trouble in the last year or so, but none of that has been Lance's fault. A lot of it has been festering for years, well before Lance became sheriff. Shep knows that, but he has to blame someone for his loss."

"I see. Well, maybe Lance can redeem himself in his deputy's eyes if he's finally able to bring charges against my mother's killer."

"I doubt it," Omar said. "But you're not doing this for Lance, and certainly not for Shep."

That was true. She was doing this for her mother and her father. And for herself. They all deserved answers.

Karine slid the papers out of the file and passed the reports on top to Omar. "Why don't you start with this top half and I can start with the bottom half."

They dug into their respective files, reading quietly for the better part of an hour. From all appearances, the investigation into her mother's death had been thorough. The sheriff had talked to several of her mom and dad's friends, neighbors and coworkers. No one had seemed to have any idea who could have attacked her mother, or why.

It was also clear from the file that the police had suspected her father. They'd questioned him multiple times and looked into his finances. Although there was never any evidence that he'd had a hand in his wife's death, some of the handwritten notes by then sheriff Edward Sampson revealed an open skepticism. One word in particular caught Karine's eye.

Affair.

"Does the former sheriff still live in Carling Lake?" Karine asked Omar.

Omar shook his head. "No. He moved to Phoenix when he retired. Why?"

Karine pointed to the word *affair* in the notes she'd been reading. "I'd like to ask him what he meant when he wrote this note. 'Affair.' Probably another one of the rumors going around about why my father would have killed my mother," she said disdainfully.

"Do you know if your father was having an affair?" Omar asked gently.

"It's not exactly a topic that's come up between me and Dad. You know he doesn't like to talk about Mom, her murder, or Carling Lake at all, really."

Omar set the report he had been reading aside. "You know, if you really want to get to the bottom of things, you're going to have to find a way to get your father to talk to you. He's the only person who knows what was going on inside his marriage at the time your mother was killed. And he probably knows much more than he realizes."

She knew Omar was right. Over the years, she'd tried half a dozen times or more to get her father to open up about her mother's murder. Each of her attempts had only led to an argument and hard feelings. She loved her father; he was the only parent she had left, but his refusal to answer her questions about her mother's homicide had put a wall between them, especially since there was so much she couldn't seem to remember about that night herself.

Karine flipped to the next page in the sheriff's notes. It was a hand-drawn map of the first floor of her childhood home. Squares marked where the furniture had sat twenty-three years earlier. An X marked the spot where her mother's body had been found in the hallway between the living room and the kitchen.

Karine put the notes aside and reached for another file from the accordion folder Deputy Bridges had given them, regretting it almost immediately.

Inside were photographs of the crime scene. She gasped.

Omar looked over and, seeing the photos in her hand, reached for them. "You don't have to look at these."

Karine pulled the photos away before he could take them from her hands. "No. I want… I need to see them."

There were several photos of her mother's body from various angles. If she had known any better, she might've convinced herself that her mother had simply decided to take a nap on the floor. But the dark purple marks marring her neck and the blood put truth to that lie. She couldn't imagine what her mother must have felt as she'd faced her killer. Had she known she only had moments left to live? Had she feared her daughter, asleep in her bed upstairs, would be next? She knew that her mother had fought for her life. The police report had indicated Marilee had several chipped fingernails. So far, Karine hadn't found a DNA report in the file, leaving open the question of whether one had been ordered.

After a moment more, she stuffed the photos back into the file folder and slid it across the table. "I don't need to see any more."

Omar ran a hand down her back. "We can leave whenever you're ready. You don't have to do this all today."

She knew Omar wanted to say she didn't have to do this at all. She couldn't really expect him to understand, even if he was her best friend. It wasn't something anyone could understand unless they'd been through it themselves.

The door to the room crashed open.

Omar was on his feet in a flash, putting his body between her and the interloper.

Karine leaned around Omar to see who had burst in, although she had a feeling she knew who it was before her eyes landed on the person. She was right.

Deputy Shep Coben stood in the doorway, his face red. "What the hell do you two think you're doing?"

"We're looking at the file on Marilee Eloi's murder. The sheriff gave us permission," Omar responded.

"I don't care what Lance gave you permission to do. I'm in charge until he returns from his vacation." Shep spat *vacation* as if it was a dirty word.

From what Karine could see, he was a man in desperate need of some time away to unwind.

"And as long as I am in charge, I'm not gonna have any civilians in here compromising my investigations. It's time for you to leave unless you want me to put you in handcuffs."

Omar held up his hands. "If that's what you want, Shep, we'll leave."

Karine took the hand that Omar extended to her and let him pull her up from her chair.

Shep stepped back out of the room to let them pass. He stopped them before they got all the way out. "You two need to listen to me, and listen to me good. Stop this investigation of yours. Your mother is gone. There's nothing you can do now to help her or bring her back. I won't let you rip this town apart over something that happened more than twenty years ago."

Karine looked the deputy square in the eye. "I think a lawman would want answers to an unsolved murder that happened in his town. But whether you want answers or not, Deputy Coben, I plan to get them. And if I have to rip this town apart to do it, then so be it."

OMAR AND KARINE stepped out of the police station and headed for the parking lot.

"Well, that went well," Karine said with a heavy dose of sarcasm. "We didn't learn anything that could help us."

Omar placed a hand on her back and steered her toward their cars. "You know my job doesn't just involve finding lost campers and fining tourists for littering. There's an investigatory component too. Right now, I'm working on an investigation into possible illegal dumping and it's not going well. That's kind of how investigations are. You follow a trail and sometimes it leads to a dead end. Or nowhere. Then you have to find another. You're looking for answers that have remained hidden for twenty-three years. It's going to take time."

Karine chewed her bottom lip. "I don't have time. I only took a week off of work and you don't know how hard that was to get."

Omar hesitated to tell her how unlikely it was she'd find anything at all in a week.

"Mr. Monroe."

Omar turned to see Daton Spindler hurrying toward him and Karine. The man's sudden appearance was as much of a surprise as the fact that Daton knew his name.

Daton was the CEO of Spindler Plastics, a major employer in the surrounding area. Omar had seen him around town at various events, but the two had never spoken.

Daton came to a stop in front of them. "I'm glad I caught you. I heard Miss Eloi was in town and I'd planned to stop by and say hello."

"I'm sorry, but I don't believe we've met," Karine said.

Daton pressed his palm to his chest. "Please forgive me. We've never met, but I knew your mom. You were so young the last time I saw you, it's no surprise you don't remember me. My name is Daton Spindler. Your mom and I grew up together, and we were good friends once."

Omar shot a glance at Karine. He could tell from the look on her face she knew nothing about a friendship between her mother and Daton.

"I'm sorry, Mr. Spindler, but I don't remember much about my mother's life and Carling Lake."

"Of course not, and I don't mean to spring myself on you. Your mother was a good friend to me and I just wanted to let you know that if there is anything you need while you're in town, you just let me know."

"That's very kind of you," Karine said.

"Daton is the CEO of Spindler Plastics. His family has been a staple in Carling Lake for many generations."

"As has yours, Monroe."

Omar nodded in acknowledgment of the compliment. His family had been in Carling Lake for more than three generations, but they hadn't achieved anywhere near the social status of the Spindlers.

"It's hard to imagine you and Miss Marilee as friends," Omar said, unable to keep the suspicion out of his tone.

Daton chuckled. "I guess it is. Marilee, Amber and I went to the same primary and secondary school. We were the only two kids from Carling Lake to go to the private school in Stunnersville. It was an unlikely pairing, but it worked."

"Spindler?" Karine said, her forehead scrunched. "Were you married to Amber Burke Spindler?"

Daton shot Karine a look of surprise. "She's my ex-wife. Do you know her?"

Omar knew the look on Karine's face. There was something she didn't want to say.

"No. Not really. I just heard her name somewhere… Mr. Spindler, I'd love to sit down and talk to you sometime about my mother," Karine said, changing the topic back to Daton's friendship with her mother. "That's part of why I'm here. To learn more about my mom."

Omar was glad she hadn't added the piece about finding out who'd murdered Marilee. He was sure the news would make its way around town, but the fewer people who knew, the better, as far as he was concerned.

"Anytime," Daton said, reaching into the inside pocket of his suit and pulling out a business card. He passed it to Karine. "And please, it's just Daton. Everybody just calls me Daton."

"Daton then. I'll give you a call soon."

"I'll be looking forward to it," Daton said with a wide smile. "Mr. Monroe." Daton nodded then turned on his heel and strode away.

"That was…" Karine started.

"Strange," Omar finished.

"Yes. Strange. He doesn't seem like the type of man my

mom would have been friends with. She was very artsy and into nature. I can't see her being friends with someone who's built a fortune on producing plastic."

Omar watched Daton get into a black Porsche parked at the corner.

"To be fair, Daton Spindler simply inherited the company. His family had probably assumed from the moment he was born that he'd take over the reins of the family business. He may not have felt like he had much choice in the matter."

"Maybe," Karine said, dropping the business card into her purse. "I still find it interesting. And I definitely want to sit down and talk to him soon."

"Hey, what was that about Amber Spindler? How do you really know her?"

Karine fiddled with the automatic door opener for her car and avoided his gaze. "What do you mean? I said I heard her name somewhere."

"You've been in town for less than a day."

Karine remained silent.

"Karine—"

"Okay, look..." She looked at him. "Amber emailed me a few weeks ago. She said she had something to tell me about my mother."

"I can't believe you didn't tell me."

"Amber asked me not to tell anyone. I'm meeting her at her house this afternoon."

"Not without me."

She put a hand to his chest. "Yes, without you. That's the way she wants it and I'm not going to do anything that could make her change her mind about telling me whatever it is she wants to tell me."

He frowned. “I don’t like it.”

“You don’t have to. I know you want to help, but I have to do this part on my own.”

He let out a frustrated sigh. “You’ll call me as soon as you leave her house, and if you get a negative vibe at all, you’ll get out of there immediately.”

She grinned. “Negative vibe. Run. Got you.”

He didn’t respond to her attempt to inject some levity into the conversation. “Karine, I’m serious. Until we have answers, you can’t trust anyone in Carling Lake.”

Chapter Four

Omar followed her back to her house.

Karine opened her front door and they stepped inside, her nerves prickling. It had been dark and she'd been tired when she'd gotten to the house the night before. She'd stayed downstairs long enough to make herself a quick PB&J and then headed up to grab some shut-eye. Of course then she'd been attacked and she hadn't slept much at all after Omar and Deputy Coben left. When she'd woken this morning, she had been in a rush to make it to the diner to meet up with Lance and Omar.

But now she took in her childhood home. The furniture was completely different, and although she couldn't remember the days and weeks surrounding her mother's death, she could remember the many happy years she and her parents had spent together in the house before the tragedy. She closed her eyes and could almost smell her mother's famous cinnamon-and-sugar cookies baking in the oven. Her father hadn't had a proper office. Instead, he'd pushed a desk into the far corner of the living room, where she would often find him reading his botany journals or grading papers.

They'd had a big brown sofa that sat in the middle of the living room opposite an old boxy television set. Her mother had loved having family Friday movie and popcorn nights. Even her always-serious father had seemed to loosen up on movie night.

All the furniture now was functional and neutral. Perfectly acceptable for the renters who'd lived in the house in the ensuing years and nothing that anyone would get upset about if it got broken.

Now that she had seen the photos of the house as a crime scene, she couldn't get the picture of her mother lying in the space between the living room and the kitchen out of her head.

"Are you okay?" Omar asked.

"I knew my mother died in this house, but those pictures… Now I can't get the image out of my head."

Omar turned her to face him and lightly grasped her shoulders. "You know you don't have to stay here, right? You can stay at my house. I have a guest room."

Karine shook her head. "No, I need to be here. Hopefully, being in this space will jog my memories. I need to know what's real and what's not."

"You know, we've spoken generally about the night your mother died, but you've never spoken to me about the details of that night." Omar led her to the sofa and they sat. "I don't want to push you, but it might help."

"You're not pushing me. And you should know at least as much as I know if you're going to help me get answers."

"I plan to be right by your side," he said, wrapping an arm around her shoulder.

A warmth pushed through her at his touch. It gave her the strength to resist the memories of the worst day of her life.

"Like I said, I don't remember much. At least, I didn't remember much before the last couple of months. I'd been starting to have dreams, dreams where I saw my mom lying on the floor and the blood, a lot like in the photos we saw at the police station. But the dreams are much more vivid."

"You think you saw your mother that night?"

"I'm not sure. My dad never told me much, but he did tell me that when he came home and found my mom, he went straight to my room and found me still asleep. He said he threw a blanket over my head so I wouldn't see anything while he carried me down the stairs and out of the house."

"Maybe the blanket slipped? Maybe you did accidentally get a peek at your mom before your dad got you out of the house?"

Karine pulled away enough to look up at Omar sitting next to her. "I don't think so." She shook her head. "In my dream, I see my mom lying on the floor in the hall, but there's also someone else there. A shadow."

She could tell from the look on his face he wasn't sure.

"Our minds can play tricks on us. Just because you see a shadow in your dream doesn't mean one was there."

She stayed quiet.

She understood where he was coming from, and certainly with his law enforcement background and experience, he was probably right, but her gut told her that the shadowy person she saw in her dreams was her mother's killer. But Omar wasn't wrong. Her gut wasn't evidence.

"All I'm saying is that we have to keep an open mind if we want to get answers."

"What do you plan to do now?" Omar asked, rising from the sofa.

She stood too.

"I'm not sure. I'm meeting Amber Spindler this afternoon, but I don't have anything I have to do until then. Don't you have to go to work?"

"I do, but I want to make sure you aren't going to get yourself into any trouble."

Karine eyeballed the ceiling. "I'm not planning on getting into any trouble. Actually, I think the combination of jet lag and drama is starting to hit me. I want to take a nap and I haven't had a moment to unpack fully and settle in." She was emotionally and physically exhausted from the last couple of days.

Omar cupped her cheek. "Going through that file had to be emotionally taxing. Why don't you take a break? Unpack. Unwind. And let me take you out for dinner tonight. We can catch up."

She felt the corners of her mouth edge up and excitement buzzed through her. "Unpacking and rest will have to wait. I'm meeting Amber Spindler at her place this afternoon."

Omar's hand dropped to his side. "Are you sure it's a good idea to meet Amber alone?"

She smiled. "I'll be fine. She was my mother's best friend. But dinner sounds great."

He returned her smile. "It's a date then."

Chapter Five

The ranger's station was located in a long, narrow clapboard structure topped with cedar-shake shingles. It was just after noon and Omar stood in the station's conference room, next to Ranger Emmanuel Pearson. Emmanuel had been hired recently in a part-time capacity, which had helped ease Omar's ever-increasing workload. Carling Lake Forest State Park was three hundred acres of forestland that saw thousands of tourists each year. As a ranger, he dealt with everything from bear sightings and lost hikers to the occasional small-time drug bust.

At the moment, he and Emmanuel were staring at a map of the forest that Omar had pinned to the bulletin board and which denoted areas where he suspected an unknown contaminant was polluting the water source. Colored pins marked areas where he'd found dead birds and smaller woodland creatures. He'd highlighted in yellow the streams that had been tested and come back clear of any outside pollutants. There didn't seem to be any rhyme or reason to what he'd been seeing, and yet his gut told him there was something there. If some sort of contaminant was working its way through the forest and he didn't find its source, there was a good likelihood that larger animals could become affected and then, possibly, humans.

"I'm thinking maybe I'll take a trip up here on my day off this week." Omar pointed to the northernmost section of the forest on the map, where there was a cluster of pins. "See if I find anything suspicious or unusual."

"Haven't you already been up there looking for clues?" Emmanuel questioned.

"Yeah, but I only tested these water bodies here." He pointed to the highlighted areas. "John only authorized enough money for limited testing and I had to make a judgment call about where to test. Maybe I chose wrong. I want to run tests on water bodies further away. See if anything pops."

His theory was that something was tainting a water source, obviously not the streams he'd already had tested, but there were dozens of little creeks and streams that ran through the forest, not to mention the ephemeral creeks and streams. Maybe one of those smaller water bodies was the source of the toxin. Based on the placement of the clusters on his map, contaminated water was going to be the most likely source. Assuming he was right about a pollutant at all and that he'd identified all the affected areas. Big assumptions, he knew, but he had to start somewhere.

"What is going on here?"

Omar and Emmanuel turned. Their boss was standing in the doorway of the conference room.

Emmanuel visibly gulped, shooting a nervous glance at Omar.

Omar and John Huyton had gotten off on the wrong foot from the first day Omar had transferred to Carling Lake.

At his last post, his regional supervisor had trusted the rangers on the ground to know their territory. Whenever there'd been a problem, his supervisor had provided whatever resources and support he could to the rangers to solve it quickly and with as little upheaval to the environment as possible. He'd let the rangers do their jobs. In fact, Omar couldn't remember a single time when his prior supervisor had showed up at the station unannounced.

But John was the opposite. His unannounced visits were close to becoming a habit, and he seemed to think his sole job was to keep an eye on the budgetary bottom line. Omar knew that the overall budget for state parks was perpetually on the chopping block and grew smaller and smaller each year. But his job wasn't about money. It was about preserving the beautiful, majestic land that was the Carling Lake Forest State Park for the generations that would follow.

John didn't see it that way though.

Omar had fought tooth and nail to get John to authorize the initial testing of the four streams he'd identified as potentially contaminated. When those tests had come back showing no problem, John had considered the matter closed. No amount of discussion had convinced him to authorize more testing of the water bodies and the continued search for an answer for what Omar was seeing on the ground. The last time Omar had broached the topic of a possible pollutant or contaminant affecting certain of the small creatures in the woods, John had yelled that the matter was closed, that there was no way more testing would be approved, and that Omar should stop wasting his time.

So he'd gone rogue. Paying out of his own pocket for water testing was expensive, but he'd resolved to do it, and it didn't cost him anything to keep his eyes open and map out the areas where he was finding the affected animals. Nor did it cost him anything to ask a few discreet questions. There was a mining operation about forty miles west of Carling Lake, and although the regulations around mining were strict, it wouldn't be the first time a big corporation had sought to cut corners and, accidentally or on purpose, caused damage to the surrounding environment. So far, though, his questions had turned up nothing useful. And now it looked like he was going to have to answer for ignoring his boss's order to stand down.

John plunked his hands on his hips. "I asked what's going on here? What is this?" He gestured toward the map.

"It's a map of the areas where I've found the remains of several small birds, squirrels, and other small animals," Omar answered resolutely.

John's face pinked. "I want to talk to you in your office, Monroe. Now." John spun on his heel and marched from the room toward Omar's office.

Emmanuel gave him a sympathetic look, but made no move to follow.

That was fine. Omar was the senior ranger and this off-the-books investigation was his baby. If someone was going to get called out over it, it should be him.

John was pacing the small office when Omar entered, which basically meant he took two steps forward before he was forced to turn and take two steps back. It hardly seemed worth the effort, but John had always struck Omar as more show than substance.

"I thought I made myself clear that you needed to drop this idea that there was some sort of contaminate affecting the Carling Lake Forest." John ceased pacing, but he blocked the path to the desk and forced Omar to stay standing.

Omar stood by the door, his back straight. John was, at best, five foot six, which meant Omar had about six inches on him. He used that advantage now, literally looking down on his boss.

"You did. But part of my job is to identify and document abnormalities in my coverage area. That's what I'm doing. My job," he emphasized.

"Abnormalities," John snapped. "You did the tests. Expensive tests, I'd add, and they came back clear. There are no abnormalities."

"Maybe not in the water that was tested, but something is going on here. I want to make sure I stay on top of it."

A dark red hue climbed up John's neck. "You are bordering on insubordination here, Monroe. I told you to drop this and that's what I meant. Drop. It. Now. Or I will write you up."

"Sir," Omar said through clenched teeth, "I don't think you understand—"

"I understand perfectly," John boomed. "And I am in charge. Now, have I made myself clear on this issue?"

Omar's temper festered, but he kept it in check. John may be a bureaucratic hack who only cared about money, but he was still the boss.

"Understood."

"Good." John gave him a weaselly smile. He took a step forward and Omar moved out from in front of the door so he could get by. With his hand on the doorknob, John turned. "I'll check in with you later this week. I want to see things back on track in this office or I'll have to take more serious measures."

John walked out, leaving Omar staring after him, wondering if his supervisor's eagerness to nip his investigation in the bud was solely due to budgetary concerns or if there was something else, something more nefarious, behind his threats.

Chapter Six

Karine drove to Amber's house, passing through downtown Carling Lake. The town had changed over the years, but there was enough left of the Carling Lake that she remembered to conjure a sense of déjà vu. She came to a stop at an intersection at the center of town. The storefronts had been modernized, and there were several shop names that she didn't recognize, but the ice cream shop was still there, as was the *Carling Lake Weekly*, although the art gallery next to it had not been there when she was a kid. "The West Gallery" she read on the discreet lettering scrolling across the bottom of the glass window. James West's place. She would have to make sure she stopped in.

The car behind her honked and she pressed down on the accelerator, driving through the intersection.

She reached Mockingbird Estates and made a right into a newish upper-class neighborhood. Each of the houses was two to three stories and set far enough apart from one another to afford the occupants quite a bit of privacy. Despite the size and undoubtedly the cost, many of the homes looked to be unoccupied, which didn't surprise her. The heart of Carling Lake was its dedicated year-round citizenry, but the town relied on its seasonal residents and tourists for survival.

Karine turned onto a wide cul-de-sac and parked in front of the address that Amber had given her. There were no lights on in the house, but a Lexus SUV was parked in the driveway.

She checked the email from Amber: 2:30 p.m. She was right on time.

She got out of the car as a gust of wind, whooshing off the nearby lake, blew past. She yanked her arm clear of the car before the door slammed shut on it and pulled the collar of her light jacket tightly around her. It was mid-September, but she'd forgotten that fall came more quickly in the mountains. The heavy, dark gray clouds overhead didn't help. They cast a melancholy pallor over the morning. It smelled like rain, as her father often said. She still didn't know what rain smelled like, but she knew she'd have to put "buy a heavier jacket" on her list of things to do.

She made her way to the front of the house and rang the doorbell.

No answer.

A chill that had nothing to do with the wind engulfed her. Something was wrong. The house was too still.

She peeked through the front window to the left of the door. The dining room was empty.

She moved to the window to the right of the door and spied a couch, coffee table and television set. A leather handbag sat on the coffee table. So, Amber was home. No woman would go anywhere without her purse.

Karine rang the bell again. Minutes passed and still no answer.

She debated leaving, but Amber knew she was coming, and her email had been so imploring. Maybe she was in the shower or... Amber lived alone and hadn't Karine read that most household accidents happened in the bathroom? Or was that the kitchen? Either way, Amber could need medical attention.

She bounded down the porch steps and rounded the house. The side door into the garage was locked, so she kept moving toward the back of the house.

The front porch on the home had been just big enough for one person to stand there while waiting to be let in. But Amber had gone all out in building the back porch. It extended a good nine feet and ran the width of the house. She had set one side up as an outdoor living room while the other side resembled an outdoor kitchen, complete with a built-in barbecue and pizza oven. A series of French doors ran across the back of the house, letting in an abundance of natural light.

Karine climbed the porch steps and peered through the glass in the door.

Nothing looked out of place in the kitchen. Her gaze traveled to the adjacent den, which had been decorated with a nautical theme. Blues and greens abounded—the sofa, the rugs, the walls. A painting of the ocean hung over the fireplace, and an intricate model boat held a prominent place on a center table.

She was just about to admit defeat and head home when her eyes fell on something that froze her in place.

A hand hung off the side of the sofa, fingers skimming the ocean-blue rug.

Her heart raced. “Amber! Amber, it’s Karine Eloi. Amber!” She banged on the French doors.

The figure on the sofa didn’t move. In fact, whoever was lying there was unnaturally still.

She tried the door’s handle, unconcerned with the impoliteness of simply walking into Amber’s home.

The doorknob turned, and she let herself into the house, rushing to the sofa.

Any hope she’d had that Amber was just a very heavy sleeper was immediately dashed.

Amber’s eyes stared, unseeing, at the seafoam-colored ceiling. A bottle of vodka and a glass sat on the coffee table in front of the sofa. A small orange pill bottle peeked out from under the sofa. Diazepam, she read on its label.

Whatever Amber had wanted to tell her, she’d taken it to her grave.

Her heart still pounding furiously, Karine reached for her phone. On instinct, she called the one person she knew she could count on.

“Karine, hey.” Omar’s deep baritone carried over the phone. “Are you done with your meeting with Amber Burke Spindler already? What did she want to tell you?”

“I don’t know… I…” Karine fought to catch her breath.

“Karine? Are you okay? What’s wrong? Where are you?”

“Amber’s house. She’s… Omar, she’s dead.”

“Are you still in the house?”

“Yes, I’m… It looks like she overdosed.”

“Karine, get out of the house. Get back in your car and lock the doors. Do it now.”

She backed away from the sofa and hurried through the French doors and across the yard, back to her car. She could hear Omar on another line talking, requesting an ambulance and the sheriff's deputy be dispatched to Amber's house in the Mockingbird Estates.

"Omar, I've got her exact address," she said, locking the car doors while rattling off the address.

Omar repeated the address to the person he was speaking with, then came back on the phone line. "Karine, I'm on my way. Stay in your car until the sheriff's office gets there."

"Okay." The little shred of sunlight that had managed to pierce the dark skies suddenly vanished. Thunder rolled in the distance as a fat raindrop landed on her windshield. "Omar, hurry."

OMAR BARELY SLOWED long enough to tell Emmanuel where he was headed. His state-issued pickup didn't have flashers and sirens like the sheriff's department vehicles, but it was the offseason and midafternoon traffic was light. The rain seemed to be helpfully holding off for the most part. Only a few stray raindrops fell as he raced toward Amber Spindler's house.

He made it to Mockingbird Estates in record time, but not fast enough to beat Deputy Coben.

He turned the corner leading onto Amber Spindler's cul-de-sac and spied the deputy talking to Karine next to her car.

He was out of the truck and racing to her side a split second after throwing his pickup into Park.

"Are you okay?" He pulled Karine into his arms, completely unconcerned about interrupting the conversation between her and the deputy.

"I'm okay. Shaken, but okay." He bet. Given what she'd

told him about her recently resurfaced memories of finding her mother, finding another body had to have been traumatic.

"Excuse me, Mr. Monroe. I was interviewing a witness. You can wait over there—" Shep pointed to the pickup "—until I'm done."

Omar kept one arm wrapped around Karine and glared at the deputy. He wasn't going to leave Karine's side.

Shep glared back.

After a long moment, Karine sighed. "Deputy Coben, can we please just get on with it? I'd like to leave sometime today."

Shep shifted his glare to Karine. "Fine." He looked down at the notepad in his hand. "I believe you'd just gotten to the point in your story where you arrived at the house when we were interrupted."

"Right, I rang the doorbell, but Amber didn't answer. I could see her purse in the living room through the front window, and her car was in the driveway."

"So you just traipsed around to the back of her house? You really must have wanted to speak with her."

"Amber asked me to come over at two thirty. She had something important she wanted to tell me. I thought she might have been in the shower or maybe she'd fallen or something and couldn't get to the door."

Shep harrumphed. "Well, that wasn't a bad theory. Everybody around these parts knows that Amber imbibes too frequently for her own good and that she has a problem with pills. Chews them like candy."

Unfortunately, the deputy wasn't exaggerating. Amber had been on a downward spiral ever since Daton had left her for a much younger executive at his plastics company three years earlier. The gossip mill had long churned around the fact that Amber hadn't been able to give Daton the heirs he'd so desperately wanted. The new wife's pregnancy and the birth of twin boys last year had only seemed to accelerate Amber's decline.

"What did Amber want to talk to you about?" Shep pressed.

Karine shot a look at Omar. After a decades-long friendship, he didn't need to say anything to convey a message.

Karine turned back to Shep. "I don't know. She didn't get a chance to tell me."

The deputy's eyes narrowed to slits. He had undoubtedly surmised that whatever Amber had wanted to tell Karine might have to do with Marilee's death. And since Shep had made no secret about how he felt about Karine's investigation into her mother's death, it made sense that Karine would want to keep as much information as close to her vest as possible.

"Okay." Shep eyed them both with unabashed hostility. "Continue."

Karine recounted how she'd gone around back, had seen a hand hanging off the sofa through the French doors and, after finding the doors unlocked, had gone inside to see if she could help the person. But Amber had been beyond help.

"We'll have to wait for the medical examiner to know for sure, but I've seen a few overdoses in my time on the force. It looks like there was nothing you could have done for her," Shep said in a rare show of sensitivity. "She probably expired sometime last night."

Karine shook her head. "It doesn't make any sense. I mean, she knew I was coming to see her this afternoon."

Shep removed his hat and swiped his sleeve across his forehead. Despite the cool air, the beads of sweat congregated at his hairline. "Might not have been intentional. Someone as used to taking pills and drinking as much as Amber was…constantly need to increase their usage to get the desired effects. Her poor body just probably couldn't take any more."

"Shep, if you've got what you need, I'd like to take Karine home now," Omar said.

"Yeah, sure." Shep waved a hand absently. "As I'm sure you know, her car has to stay here. Part of the scene. Probably release it sometime this afternoon or evening. I'll call you when it's clear for you to come by and pick it up."

Karine nodded. "Thank you, Deputy."

Omar pulled Karine closer to his side. She was trembling slightly, and he wasn't sure it was due to the flimsy jacket she wore. They turned toward his pickup.

"Ms. Eloi," Shep called.

They turned back in unison.

The deputy's eyes had narrowed into beady little slits. "You aren't planning to leave town anytime soon, are you? I might have more questions for you."

Omar guessed it was too much to expect Shep to be decent for more than a minute or two at a time.

"I plan to be here for the rest of the week."

Shep nodded before turning and stomping up the walk to the house.

Karine twisted in Omar's arms, looking up at him.

"Does that mean Deputy Coben hasn't one hundred percent bought into the theory that Amber accidentally overdosed?"

"I don't know about Shep, but I sure don't. Let's get out of here. We need to talk."

MARILEE'S KILLER WATCHED the commotion at Amber's place from the shadows of a vacant house across the street. No one noticed. The killer was good at going unnoticed. Always had been.

Amber. It was a shame, but had to be done. The killer thought Amber's silence had been bought long ago, but you really couldn't trust anyone nowadays. Amber had suffered the consequences of her attempted treachery.

But it still felt like the secrets of the past were bubbling to the surface now, and the killer wasn't sure what to do about it. One thing was for certain, the killer hadn't spent the last twenty-three years covering their tracks to fail now.

Hopefully, all Karine Eloi needed was a warning.

Hopefully for her, that was.

Chapter Seven

Omar drove her back to her house. As soon as she got inside, she put the electric teakettle on.

"You are buying Deputy Coben's theory that Amber overdosed, are you?"

"It's possible," Omar answered.

Karine frowned at him. Lots of things were possible, but plausible? She wasn't buying the accidental overdose line.

"It is, Karine." Omar sat at the kitchen table. "Amber had a problem. We all knew it, even if most of us preferred to look away," he added sadly.

Karin grabbed the kettle when it started to whistle. She poured the boiling water into two cups and added tea bags. "Okay, but don't you think that makes it less likely that she would accidentally overdose? I mean, if she abused drugs and alcohol regularly, she probably knew how much she could handle." She carried the cups to the table, sliding a mug of hot tea across the surface to Omar.

He wrapped both hands around the warm mug. "By that logic, no one would ever accidentally overdose, and we know that's not the case."

That drew another frown, yet she had to concede the point.

"But I can't say I don't have my suspicions. The timing

is just too coincidental for me. Especially following the break-in at your house the other night."

"Exactly." Karine punctuated the word by pointing at him.

Omar gave her a searching look over the top of his mug. "Don't tell me you plan on investigating Amber's death now too?"

"To the extent that it might answer some questions about my mother's, yes. There is something going on here. I'm not sure what, or why, but I feel like it's now or never for getting answers about my mother's murder."

Omar sighed heavily. "How do you plan on doing that?"

"Well, Daton used to be married to Amber. Maybe he has some idea about what she wanted to tell me."

"Maybe." Omar looked skeptical. "Daton and Amber's divorce wasn't amicable though. I doubt she would have confided in him."

"Is there anyone she would have confided in? A friend or family member?"

Omar shook his head slowly, thinking. "Amber has been kind of a loner since the divorce. She used to attend all the social functions, fundraisers and such for the church, and she chaired the Carling Lake Winter Festival during the years Spindler Plastics was the lead sponsor. But the divorce knocked her down a few rungs on the social ladder." He thought for a minute. "She does employ Fiona Kessler to clean for her a few times a week. I think I've seen them having coffee together at the café in town once or twice."

"Okay, Fiona Kessler. It's someplace to start at least."

Omar stood. "I have to get back to work. Are we still on for dinner tonight?"

She hesitated for a moment. It somehow seemed wrong to be making dinner plans when a woman had just died. But she and Omar would have to eat no matter what. And if she were honest, she was looking forward to dinner with Omar more than she probably should be. "Yeah, we're still on."

It was Omar's turn to smile. "Good. I'll pick you up at eight."

SHE ANSWERED THE door to Omar at exactly 8:00 p.m.

He'd changed out of his work clothes and into black slacks and loafers and a burgundy-satiny button-down shirt. It looked like he'd taken the time to shape up his goatee and the scent of his aftershave went straight to her core. She'd always known her best friend was good-looking, but the man standing in front of her wasn't just attractive. He was sexy.

"You look great," he said, giving her a brilliant smile that sent butterflies fluttering in her stomach.

She wasn't wearing anything fancy, a blue-and-white-flowered sundress that hit just above the knees and sandals, but she heated under his appreciative gaze.

"So do you." She locked the door and followed him past her rental, which she'd picked up once Shep had called to tell her he was releasing the crime scene, to Omar's pickup.

"There are a bunch of new fancy restaurants in town since you've last been here, but I figured you might appreciate just going back to our old haunts, so I plan to take you to Barney's Bar and Grill, if that's okay?"

"That's great. My parents used to take me to Barney's for special occasions."

Barney's parking lot was full when they arrived, but the

hostess promised it would only be a couple minutes' wait while a table was cleared for them.

Karine excused herself to the ladies' room while they waited. As she made her way back to Omar, an older man with thinning brown hair and striking gray eyes homed in on her as she passed the bar. He looked vaguely familiar, yet the curl of his lips and the hatred in his eyes had her quickening her steps.

"Who's that man sitting on the third stool from the left at the bar?" she asked when she returned to Omar's side.

He turned and focused on where she'd indicated.

The man still stared unabashedly.

"That's Martin Howser. He used to be the high school principal at Carling Lake High. I guess he recognizes you as Marilee's daughter."

"I guess."

The man turned his back to them.

The hostess gestured for them to follow her then, and Karine put the man out of her head. Some people might not want her back in town dredging up old memories, but they'd have to deal with it. They settled into their table and perused the menu.

"Omar Monroe. Long time no see."

Karine looked up at the waitress who had stopped at the edge of the table. It took a moment for her to put a name to the face. Blanca Coben.

Omar shot Blanca a brief, polite smile. "Hi, Blanca. I've been pretty busy at work. I've been getting off too late to come to the restaurant for dinner."

Blanca ran her finger lightly across Omar's shoulder. "Now you know I'm here to serve you whenever you need."

That comment was overloaded with sexual innuendo.

The tips of Omar's ears reddened in embarrassment and he looked down at the menu in his hand.

Karine fought the urge to slap Blanca's finger away from Omar's shoulder.

Blanca, the head mean girl at Carling Lake middle school during Karine's brief tenure there, had grown up. And from the looks of it, life had not treated her kindly. Blanca was skinnier than looked healthy and the smell of stale beer permeated from her body. Although the light in the room was dim, Karine could see that Blanca's eyes were bloodshot and her skin sallow.

"Blanca. It's been a long time." She couldn't say she really cared about the answer, but the question had the desired effect of pulling Blanca's attention away from Omar.

Blanca's smile dimmed considerably. "Karine Eloi. I heard you were back in town stirring up trouble."

She had no doubt Blanca had gotten that misleading piece of gossip from her uncle, Deputy Shep Coben.

Not taking Blanca's bait, Karine plastered a smile on her face. "How have you been, Blanca?"

Blanca snapped the gum in her mouth. "I'm just fine. Working. Taking care of my kids and my mother. It's not a fancy Los Angeles life, but it suits me just fine."

"Blanca," Omar said with a warning in his voice.

Blanca turned a smile on Omar. "Oh, Omar, I'm sure a big-city girl like Karine knows I am just teasing her."

"Well, stop teasing."

"It's fine, Omar," Karine said. She could tell by the look in his eyes that it was not fine with him.

"I think we'd like to order our drinks now?" Omar said pointedly.

Karine ordered a wine spritzer and Omar got a beer.

"She likes you," Karine said after Blanca sashayed away to put in the drink orders. She hoped Omar hadn't heard the touch of jealousy that seemed to her to have rung so loudly in her words.

Omar made a face. "Blanca is not my type."

Karine smiled. "Okay. Well, I haven't heard you mention a date and I don't know how long. So, what is your type?"

Omar arched his brow. "I could say the same about you. What's your type?"

You.

She gave herself a mental shake. Where did that come from? Omar was her friend. Just her friend. Although, if she could find a man as kind, caring and funny as he was who lived in Los Angeles, she might just marry him.

"Karine? Where'd you go?"

"Sorry. A work thing just popped into my head." A blush heated her cheeks.

Blanca returned with Omar's beer and her wine spritzer. She set the drinks down on the table in front of them with a sexy smile for Omar and not so much as a glance for Karine. She left a second time with a promise to return in a moment to take their food orders.

"Here are the rules for the night," Omar said, raising his beer.

Karine picked up her glass. "There are rules for the night?"

"There are now. Rule one, no talking about or thinking about work for either of us."

"That's a rule I can get behind." Karine held her glass up higher.

"Rule two, no investigation talk."

She tapped her glass against his bottle. "Agreed."

They drank on it.

"I do have a question though," Karine said. "What are we supposed to talk about?"

"We've been friends for over thirty years—"

"Hold on there. Your family moved in when you were six, so it's just shy of thirty years. Don't make us older than we are."

Omar held up his hands with a laugh. "My apologies. Just shy of thirty years. My point is still valid. We should be able to find something to talk about besides work and murder. I, for one, want to circle back to this question of your type of man."

"I thought we were talking about your kind of woman." Were they flirting with each other? This felt like flirting, but to tell the truth, it had been so long since she'd been on a date that she wasn't sure. Not that this was a date, so it probably wasn't flirting. Probably.

Omar took another pull from his beer. His gaze locked on her face. "My kind of woman is intelligent, funny and slightly sarcastic. She's always thinking of others and has a strong sense of justice and right and wrong that guides her."

Something in Karine's belly fluttered. That had definitely seemed like flirting. It felt as if Omar was directing his words specifically to her, but he couldn't be describing her. Could he?

"A woman who, when she turns her beautiful brown

eyes on me, it feels as if I've won the greatest lottery in the world," he added, his voice low and husky.

They stared at each other for a long moment. Karine's heart raced. Despite all the people in the restaurant, the music coming from the speakers, the laughter and chatter swirling all around them, it felt like they were the only two people in the room. Maybe in the world at that moment.

"What can I get y'all?" Blanca popped up next to the table with an order pad and pen in her hand.

Barney's wasn't fancy, but they boasted the best seafood platter in town. They ordered one to share.

Karine was glad to see that the charge bouncing between them before Blanca arrived to take their orders was gone by the time she left.

They drank and chatted, catching up on the little details of their lives that had escaped telling in their phone calls and emails over the last six months. When the food arrived, they dug in. Lots of things may have changed in Carling Lake over the years, but Barney's seafood platter wasn't one of them. It was still amazingly good.

Barney's had expanded since she'd last been there to include a space at the back of the dining area for live entertainment and dancing. There wasn't a live band this night, but that hadn't kept many of the diners from taking to the dance floor and grooving to the music coming through the bar and grill's overhead speakers.

"Want to dance?" Omar asked after Blanca had cleared their empty dinner plates.

"Oh, no, I—"

Omar's eyebrow quirked up. "You've been tapping your foot and chair dancing since we sat down."

"Well, the music isn't half bad," she conceded.

"Come on." Omar stood and reached out his hand.

She gave in, taking his hand.

Mariah Carey's "Always Be My Baby" played as they hit the dance floor, but after a minute, the song faded. The first chords of Richard Marx's "Right Here Waiting" sounded from the speakers.

Karine started to turn away from the dance floor, but Omar caught her hand. She let him pull her into his arms. They were one of three or four couples on the floor. They swayed to the music, his lean, hard body pressed against hers.

They'd danced together before, at parties and clubs, but this felt different. Intimate.

She folded into his masculine scent, resting her head against his chest. She was pretty sure this dance, the feelings that she was experiencing at this moment, were a terrible idea, but she didn't pull away. The song ended and she opened her eyes, looking up at Omar.

"Are you okay?" he asked, his voice husky. He appeared to have been as affected by the moment as she was.

"Fine," she answered in barely more than a whisper.

"I should take you home." Omar's eyes bore into hers.

Her breath caught in her throat and all she could do was nod.

He paid the bill and they stepped out of the restaurant into the cool night air.

HE WANTED TO kiss Karine more than he'd ever wanted anything in his life. When he'd been on that dance floor, holding her in his arms, the world had just felt right. And he was pretty sure she'd felt it too.

Omar hadn't had any intentions other than catching up with his oldest friend when he'd invited her out to dinner, but maybe it was the right time to move their relationship forward. He'd been thinking about it for…years. But he was pretty sure Karine would have run. She'd never stuck with a relationship for longer than a few months. At least, not a romantic one. But it was getting harder and harder for him to pretend he didn't have feelings for her that went far beyond friendship.

They walked across the parking lot to his truck and he unlocked the passenger's-side door first. He turned to help her into the pickup. Inches separated them. The seconds ticked by, neither of them moving, their gazes locked. And then Karine went to her toes.

His mouth touched hers. The light tanginess of lemon butter lingered on her lips. Her fingers skimmed down his arms in a touch so light he could barely feel it, which made it all the more exciting somehow.

He kept the kiss light, exploring her mouth.

Karine stepped back all too soon. Her eyes shone with surprise, desire and uncertainty.

He knew her well enough to know she'd need time to process the line they'd just crossed, so he took two steps backward, giving her space.

His eyes hooked on something over Karine's shoulder. A flash of metal. "Get down!" He grabbed Karine on instinct. They hit the ground hard enough to rattle his jaw.

The gunshot reverberated in the air around them.

He rolled, using his body to cover Karine as she cried out.

Tires squealed.

Omar raised his head, but the only thing he caught was

the flash of red taillights. No make or model of the car or the person who'd shot at them.

"Are you hurt?" He was still perched over her, but he did his best to assess whether she'd been hurt in the fall. Or, God forbid, shot.

The doors to the pub opened and several people rushed to help them up.

"The sheriff is on his way," an overweight, balding man said as he offered his hand.

Omar let the man pull him to his feet and brought Karine up with him.

Deputies Coben and Bridges arrived moments later, followed by three more deputies. Once again, he and Karine found themselves giving statements to Deputy Coben. There was no question that this hadn't been an accident. Someone had shot at them. A group of diners had been leaving the restaurant when the shots had rung out and they'd seen the whole thing, backing up his and Karine's story to the deputy.

The parking lot was a crime scene, including Omar's truck. That meant they had to wait over an hour for the deputies to finish taking photos and searching the grounds before finally giving them the okay to head home.

Karine was quiet on the drive to her house. He worried that the events of the last few days were too much for her. As much as he wanted to be near her, if she was thinking about heading back to Los Angeles… Well, that just might be the safest thing.

It seemed she did have safety on her mind, just not her own.

She turned to him when he pulled into her driveway and

shut off the engine. “I don’t want you to help me investigate my mother’s murder anymore.”

“What? Why? Are you giving up on the investigation?”

“No.” She shook her head. “I just don’t want your help. It’s too dangerous. You could have been killed tonight, and it would have been all my fault.”

“Karine—”

“No, Omar.” She unbuckled her seat belt and reached for the door handle. “I’ve made up my mind. I’m not going to let you put yourself in danger.”

She got out of the truck and headed for her house.

He got out and followed. “Karine, wait.” She kept walking. “Wait!”

She stopped. Turned. “Omar—”

“No. It’s your turn to listen.” He stepped up to her and laid his hands gently on her shoulders. “I’m not going to stop helping you, no matter what you say.”

“Omar, I can’t risk…” She stopped, choking up.

He moved a hand to her face, stroking the pad of his thumb down her soft cheek. “You’re not risking anything. I am. I know that there’s a danger here. I was there tonight and the night before, and I get it. And I appreciate your concern. I wish you had more of it for yourself.”

“If you were to get hurt, if I lost you, I don’t know what I’d do.” Her eyes shone with unshed tears.

Her words sent a flood of emotions through him. He lowered his head. “I know. I feel the same way about you. So, how about we keep doing this together? Watching each other’s backs. What do you say?”

Her mouth turned up in a smile and she squeezed his hands in return. “Okay, together.”

Chapter Eight

The high-pitched squeaking of the critters in the attic didn't keep her awake for long that night, but Karine did not find relief in sleep. In her dreams, she watched her twelve-year-old self creep down the second-floor hallway from her bedroom and peer through the stair railings. Her mother lay on the floor. *Why is Mommy sleeping on the floor?* She could hear young Karine's thoughts in her head, but she knew her mother wasn't sleeping. Her mother was dead. And the person who'd killed her was there. A shadowy form circled her mother.

She attempted to focus in on the shadow, but no matter how hard she tried, she couldn't see the person's face. But now she did see something she hadn't noticed in the dream before.

The fireplace poker.

It was in the shadowy person's hand.

Young Karine was trembling now. She shrank back, away from the railing.

The shadow turned, looked up…

Karine started awake, her heart thundering in her chest, the bedsheets twisted around her legs.

Sweat beaded on her chest and her head throbbed. She

pushed the covers aside and swung her feet to the floor, padding into the bathroom.

It wasn't the first time she'd had the dream, although being in the house where her mother had been killed seemed to have made it more potent. She'd also never seen the fireplace poker in the shadow's hand before, but that could have been a result of having viewed the crime scene photos.

It was getting harder and harder to know what part of the dream was real and what part she was filling in with what she'd learned about her mother's death.

Karine got into the shower and let the hot water wash away the dream, leaving the room in her mind to allow the memories of kissing Omar to flood in.

That kiss, which had been incredible…and a mistake.

Omar was her friend. Her best friend.

Sure, okay, there was an attraction there. They were both two healthy adults, so that wasn't unexpected, but letting that attraction take over was too much of a risk. What if they moved into the romantic zone and the relationship didn't work out? She'd lose Omar. She couldn't risk that. She didn't have a lot of people in her life who she was close to. He really was it. She needed him more as a friend than as a lover. He'd understand, right? Of course he would. He probably felt the same way. Their friendship was strong, certainly strong enough to withstand one little kiss. One little, amazing kiss.

She got out of the shower and got dressed, unsurprised to see Omar heading up the walkway toward her front door. She held the door open for him by the time he stepped on to the porch.

"I brought breakfast." He held up a white paper bag with

OrganicSandwich written across it and a carrier with a cup of coffee for him and an English breakfast tea for her.

"You may enter," she joked, stepping aside and letting him pass.

They sat at the kitchen table and dug into the bacon, egg and cheese sandwiches he'd bought.

Awkwardness and something else—maybe a touch of anticipation—lingered between them. This was what she didn't want. She didn't want to feel uncomfortable around Omar.

Omar cleared his throat. "Listen, about last night—"

"If you're worried about how I'm doing after being shot at, you don't have to," she said in a voice that was a little too loud and a little too bright to her ears.

Omar must have thought so too. He tilted his head and gave her a look filled with concern.

"I just mean I'm fine. I've never been shot at before and I hope to never be again, but I'm okay."

It was quiet for a beat. Then another.

She was pretty sure Omar's "about last night" hadn't been about the shooting but about their kiss, but she wasn't ready to talk to him about that yet.

"You're fine. Okay. What are you planning to do today then?" Omar said.

She let out a breath, relieved that he wasn't going to press the kissing issue now. "I was thinking I'd go see Fiona Kessler. Maybe she can help me figure out what Amber was planning to tell me."

Omar frowned. "Fiona is…peculiar."

"Peculiar?"

He balled up the wrapper his sandwich had come in.

"She's not particularly friendly, is all. I don't have to be at work for a couple more hours. I can go with you."

Karine gathered the trash from her breakfast and stood. "Let's go."

Omar drove them to a part of town Karine didn't remember existing when she'd lived in Carling Lake. Fiona lived in a neighborhood made up of modular homes. Fiona's was one of the larger ones, but from the grime on the siding and the dirt-packed lawn, it was clear she didn't put much care into the upkeep.

FIONA KESSLER OPENED her front door wearing a pink housecoat, bedroom slippers and a wary expression. Her expression didn't change after Omar and Karine introduced themselves.

Okay, so not the friendly chat Karine had hoped for. Direct and to the point seemed like the best way to approach the situation.

"What can I do for you?" she asked without inviting them in.

"I was hoping you'd be willing to answer a few questions about Amber Spindler," Karine said.

Fiona's eyes flicked from wary to suspicious in an instant. "Are you a reporter?"

"No. I'm…well, I'm Marilee Eloi's daughter."

Fiona didn't seem surprised by the news. "I heard you found Amber."

"I did. Amber recently reached out to me. She said she wanted to tell me something about my mother."

"I don't see how I can help you." Fiona shot an uneasy glance from Omar to Karine and back.

"I think Amber was going to tell me something about my

mother's death. I understand you and Amber were friends. You worked for her. I thought maybe she'd shared with you whatever it was she was going to tell me."

"I don't know why you'd think Amber told me anything. I cleaned her house for her. We weren't friends."

Fiona's inability to meet Karine's gaze made her question whether the older woman was telling the truth.

"Whatever it was Amber wanted to tell me seemed important. I'm pretty sure it was about my mother. Are you sure you don't have any idea what it was?"

"No."

Karine could feel the irritation rolling off Omar next to her.

"When was the last time you saw Amber?" Karine asked, keeping her tone light. They needed Fiona's cooperation. If Omar was right about Fiona's solitary lifestyle, she might have been one of the last people to see Amber alive.

"I already spoke to Deputy Coben. The last time I saw Amber was the day before…the day before you found her. I clean and cook three times a week. Monday, Thursday and Saturday."

"But I found Amber on Wednesday, which means you should have been there to clean the house on Monday, not Tuesday."

"Amber asked me to change my schedule this week. She wanted me to come on Tuesday instead of Monday."

Karine shared a quick glance with Omar before turning back to Fiona. "Did Amber tell you why?"

Fiona shook her head. "No. Not really."

"No or not really?" Omar barked.

Fiona took a step back from the door. "No."

Karine shot Omar a warning look. The last thing she wanted was for Fiona to slam the door on them.

"When you saw her, did she seem worried or upset?" Karine asked in an overly saccharine tone.

Fiona stuck her hands in the pockets of the housecoat. "Maybe. A little."

"Maybe or a little?" Omar pressed.

"Fiona." Karine jumped in to speak and hopefully cut some of the tension building. "Anything you can tell us about the last time you saw Amber, how she was, what she said, it might help us understand what happened to her."

Fiona's forehead scrunched in confusion. "What happened? I thought she took too many of those pills she likes."

"Maybe, but I'm not convinced and Deputy Coben…"

Fiona harrumphed. "Coben couldn't find his behind with a compass and a map. Has the nerve to be mad that we didn't elect him sheriff. We may be simple people in Carling Lake, but we aren't stupid."

Karine smiled. "You certainly aren't."

Fiona let out a deep sigh. "Look, I really don't know what to tell you. Amber seemed a little down. Maybe a bit agitated. She didn't tell me why but…"

"But what?"

"Amber didn't get out much, but she liked using those dating apps. You know, to meet people. Sometimes she'd meet up with some of the men online, like a video date. There was one guy lately who she seemed to like. A lot. And then he just stopped responding. What is it you young people call it? He ghosted her." Fiona chuckled. "I figured she was a little down over that, but like I told her, how much of a relationship could she really have with a person she'd never met in real life?" She shrugged.

"Did you cook for her on Tuesday?" Karine asked.

"Yes. A roast with baby potatoes, carrots and freshly baked bread."

"Do you usually make so much food just for Amber?"

Fiona tapped her chin. "No, now that you mention it. But Amber was very specific about the menu."

"Maybe she expected company," Omar said.

Fiona shrugged. "If she did, she didn't tell me. And I'd have to say that's not likely. Amber doesn't have many friends, and she rarely entertains in her home."

"Rarely, but not never," Karine persisted. This could be good. If Amber had been expecting company, that person might know what she was going to tell Karine.

Or that person could have killed her.

"Rarely. Once she had a gentleman friend from one of those apps over for dinner, but it didn't go anywhere." Fiona's puckered lips said everything about how she felt about that date.

"Okay, so it's possible Amber was entertaining on Tuesday night."

"Anything is possible. Look, I really don't know anything else and I need to go." Fiona grabbed the door and took a step back.

"Wait. Is there anything else you can think of that was different about that day? Anything at all?"

Fiona paused. "Amber had me buy wine. Really nice wine. I had to go to this fancy store in Stunnersville."

"Wine?"

"Yeah. Sixty dollars a pop and she had me buy three bottles."

Omar shifted next to her. "And that was unusual?"

"Very. Amber usually drank Scotch and soda. Vodka. Rum. Gin."

"Hard liquor," Karine summarized.

"Very hard."

It wasn't much, but it was something. "Thank you."

Fiona closed the door without another word.

Karine walked beside Omar back to his truck.

"What do you think?" Karine said once they were in the pickup.

"It is possible Amber was expecting a guest, but it's really just supposition."

"Maybe so, but it's the best lead we have right now. If we can find the person that Amber was expecting to entertain the night before she died, they may know what Amber wanted to tell me."

The wheels spun as Omar pulled them away from the curb. "That's one possibility if this person exists and if we find this person."

"And another possibility?" she asked, although she was pretty sure where Omar was going with his line of thinking.

Omar braked at a stop sign. He looked into her eyes. "The other possibility is that the person Amber had over for dinner Tuesday night killed her."

Chapter Nine

Karine spent the rest of the day fielding work emails despite being on vacation and searching Amber's social media for her mystery man. It seemed likely Amber had a date, since what Fiona had described sounded like a romantic dinner. But Karine had no luck finding the mystery man.

By the time the sun went down, she had formed a new plan. Omar was at work, which was good because Karine didn't want him in danger. Deputy Coben had been quick to proclaim that there was no foul play and to declare Amber's death an accidental overdose. His main concern had been assuring the community that he had everything in hand in Sheriff Webb's absence. He didn't care about getting to the truth, but Karine did. She was going to break into Amber's house and search for clues to what Amber had wanted to tell her and maybe figure out who her mystery man was.

She wasn't exactly sure how she was going to get into the house. The police had probably locked the back door she'd entered when she'd found Amber's body. She'd cross that bridge when she got there. If she had to, she'd break one of the windowpanes in the fancy French doors, but she was hoping to find another way in, some way that wouldn't announce she'd been there.

Karine parked two blocks away from Amber's cul-de-sac and walked to the house. She'd dressed in all black and now did her best to blend into the shadows, just in case. It was late, nearing eleven at night, but you never knew who might still be up and glancing out of their window.

All three of the houses on the cul-de-sac were dark inside. Just as when she'd been there the day before, the neighboring houses appeared occupied. Still, Karine hurried around to the back of Amber's house, where she wouldn't be seen.

Just as she'd expected, the French doors were locked this time. She fussed with them for a moment, but they didn't budge. She pulled the small pinpoint flashlight she'd brought with her from her pocket and turned it on, scanning the porch or places Amber might have hidden a key.

She tried inside and underneath the planter by the door, to no avail. Above the doorjamb and windows, and under the cushions on the patio furniture. No key.

Just about to give up and go home, her eyes landed on a garish green-porcelain frog at the center of the flower bed that circled the porch. It was the only lawn ornament and decidedly out of place in the professionally manicured yard.

She hopped down the porch stairs, pocketing the penlight.

The frog was heavy. It took both hands and a considerable amount of force, but she was able to tip it enough to catch the glint of metal pushed into the soil. A key.

Karine used her knee to balance the frog while she reached underneath and grabbed the key.

Back on the porch, she unlocked the door then hesitated for a moment.

The last time she'd let herself into Amber's house, she'd

been an invited guest, sort of, but this would be crossing a line. Trespassing. Breaking and entering. Deputy Coben was already unhappy with her. He'd probably take great joy in tossing her in jail if he caught her in Amber's house.

That was a risk she was willing to take. She had to know what it was Amber had wanted to tell her. There had to be a clue inside the house.

She pushed the door open and stepped inside. Once again, she pulled her penlight from her pocket, keeping the beam pointed downward as extra insurance against being noticed from the outside.

She had no idea what she was looking for, which made it impossible to know where to search. She wished she had insisted that Amber at least give her a hint, but she'd gone over Amber's email a dozen times and there was absolutely nothing there that pointed to what Amber had wanted to show her.

Think. Amber said she had something to show her. What could that have been? A note? A photo? The possibilities felt infinite. The only thing Karine could do was search the house, looking for anything that seemed important.

Karine moved into the living room where she remembered seeing bookshelves lining one wall. The living room faced the front of the house, but thankfully, someone had pulled the curtains on the front windows so she didn't have to worry about being seen here. Still, she turned off her flashlight and stepped close to the shelves, reading the spines of the books in the dark. A half hour of looking through and behind every book on the shelves and it was clear that whatever Amber had wanted to share with her was not there. Nothing else in the room seemed like it could be what Amber had wanted to show her either. Nothing jumped out at Karine as being in any way related to her mother's murder.

"Where else would you hide something important?" Karine whispered to herself.

To be thorough, she forced herself to look under the sofa cushions and under the sofa itself even though the memory of Amber lying there creeped her out. She searched the sofa and the area around it as quickly as she could then she moved to the formal dining room. The only place to hide anything in that room was in the sideboard, but she found nothing in there except fancy silverware and extra serving dishes. She searched the kitchen cabinets, the pantry and even the refrigerator and freezer. Nothing.

She moved back down the hall and climbed the staircase to the second floor.

Double doors at the end of the hallway marked the main bedroom. She headed for the room.

The hairs on the back of her neck stood up as she moved into the space. Instinctively, she knew that whatever Amber had planned to show her was in this room. While the other areas of the house were immaculately designed, this room actually felt lived in.

A gray, queen-size upholstered bed dominated one wall with matching, gray-washed wood nightstands on either side. The bedspread was a vibrant red and was stacked with a dozen pillows in all different sizes, shapes and colors. The matching dresser stood on the opposite wall in the space between the door leading into the en suite bathroom and the open door leading into the walk-in closet.

Karine started with the nightstands, finding one completely empty and nothing but a Dan Brown novel in the other. She checked Amber's dresser drawers quickly, feeling like a creep. The odds of finding whatever Amber had wanted to show her had been long to start with, but with every passing moment, it felt like she was just wasting her time while increasing the likelihood she'd be arrested for breaking and entering.

She stepped into the closet, looking behind Amber's clothes for a secret door or safe.

"A secret door. You're losing your mind," she whispered to herself. "No, you've lost your mind. This is crazy." She ran a hand over the neat stack of sweaters on the shelf above the hanging clothes and froze. There was something solid there between the cashmere layers.

She slipped her hand under the first sweater in the pile and pulled out a compact disc.

This had to be what Amber had wanted to show her. Why else would she have hidden the disc in her closet?

She tucked the CD under her arm and stepped out of the closet.

A bumping sound came from downstairs.

Her blood ran cold.

There was someone else in Amber's house.

Her penlight fell onto the floor with a thunk that sounded to her ears as if it reverberated around the room. Had the person downstairs heard? Did they know she was up there? Were they looking for her?

Karine grabbed the penlight and hustled back to the closet, closing the door and hunkering down in the far corner.

She heard footsteps climbing the stairs and making their way down the hall. The hinges creaked as the bedroom door opened. It sounded as if the intruder said something, but the blood pounding in her ears was too loud for her to understand the words. The intruder wasn't making much of an effort to be quiet, and that was as terrifying as anything else. Maybe he wasn't being quiet because he didn't care if she knew he was coming for her. Maybe he didn't plan to give her the opportunity to tell anyone.

Or the intruder could be Deputy Coben or another deputy. Maybe someone had seen her car or the beam from her penlight and called the sheriff's department. At this point, that would be a best-case scenario. Jail wasn't looking so bad compared to the places her mind was taking her at the moment.

Her heart thundered.

Her eyes darted around the closet for something, anything, to defend herself with, but there was nothing other than clothes and the CD she now clutched in her other hand. She realized too late that hiding in the closet with no way out hadn't been the best of ideas.

The handle on the closet twisted, the door opening slowly.

She may not have had a weapon, but that didn't mean she had to cower, waiting to be discovered. She had the element of surprise on her side.

She bounced to her feet and, with a war cry, launched herself at the figure standing in the open doorway.

She recognized Omar a millisecond before she crashed into him.

They hit the carpeted floor together, Omar on his back, she astride him.

She felt the air whoosh out of his lungs and stared down at him in stunned surprise.

They lay still for a moment, each of them appearing to be working through the shock of the moment.

"What are you doing here?" Karine finally asked.

"Looking for you."

"But why? I mean, how did you know I was here?"

"I was almost home, turning onto our street, when I saw you peeling out of your driveway and take off in the opposite direction, so I followed you. Well, I tried."

His arms were around her waist, and it felt nice. She pushed the thought aside and focused on what he was saying.

"You drive entirely too fast. You were long gone by the time I got dressed and headed out after you. I drove around town, looking for you for a bit, before I realized where you must have gone. I saw your car when I drove into the neighborhood."

So much for being stealthy.

"That still doesn't explain why you're here," she said, rolling off him and standing. She fisted her hands on her hips. "Why were you following me?"

Omar climbed to his feet. "Because I know you. I wanted to make sure you didn't get yourself in trouble, or that you had backup if you did. Remember, watching each other's backs. We agreed."

Her pique thawed a little. "I didn't want to get you in trouble if I got caught breaking in here. I knew that wouldn't be great for you with your job and all."

"Getting arrested isn't great for anyone, regardless of their job. And on that note, can we get out of here?"

Karine threw up her hands. "That's why I didn't tell you what I planned to do. I wanted to protect you."

"Thanks for that. Come on." Omar headed for the bedroom door.

"Wait." She ran back to the closet and picked up the CD where she'd dropped it.

"What is that?" Omar said, eyeing the plastic in her hands.

"I'm not sure exactly, but I found it under a sweater in Amber's closet. I'm hoping it is what she wanted to show me when she invited me over."

"Great. Not just breaking and entering, burglary. Shep will have a field day if he catches us."

"Then let's get out of here," Karine said with a smile and a sweep of her arm in the direction of the door.

Omar grumbled. "Woman, you are going to be the death of me."

Chapter Ten

Karine parked her rental in her driveway after they got back from Amber's and crossed her lawn to Omar's house.

He went straight for the fridge and grabbed a beer.

"You want one?" he offered.

She shook her head. "No. Not now."

He popped the top and took a long draft on the beer before turning back to her with narrowed eyes. "Do you have any idea how dangerous that was?"

He was furious, a rarity when it came to Karine. He could count on one hand the times he'd actually gotten angry with her over the years. She'd annoyed him for sure, but he'd always had trouble mustering real anger toward her.

That was not the case tonight. Her little stunt could have put her in real danger. But a small part of his brain also recognized that his anger wasn't just about the stunt at Amber's. He was upset that she was acting like their kiss hadn't happened. The kiss that had shaken him to his core. He knew she'd felt something, too, but she seemed intent on pretending that she hadn't.

She rolled her eyes at him. "The house was empty."

"There could have been an alarm, or a neighbor could have seen you going in. They could have called the sheriff and we already know Shep isn't the brightest bulb in the pack. He could have shown up, guns blazing."

"Whoa." She held her hands up. "You are taking this way out there. First of all, there are no neighbors. It looks like most of the houses in that fancy subdivision are owned by part-timers who hightail it out of Carling Lake after Labor Day. Second, people who hide keys under ceramic frogs don't have alarms. No one in Carling Lake has a security system, not even you, Mr. Safety," she said, pointing out the obvious. "And third, yes, if Shep had caught me I'd be in jail right now, but this isn't the Wild West and, more importantly, he didn't catch me."

"That is not the point," he replied, emphasizing each word.

"Then what is the point?" she said with exasperation. "You know I didn't ask you to come with me." She stepped up close to him and pointed a finger in his chest. "You. Followed. Me." She jabbed with each word. "You didn't have to."

He caught her finger, holding it against his chest. "I know you didn't ask me to go with you. Instead, you snuck out without me because you knew I'd tell you it was a bad idea."

A current of annoyance and something else rolled between them before she stepped back and looked away.

"I knew you would have tried to stop me. And I had to see if I could find whatever Amber wanted to show me," she said quietly.

His anger dissipated some. "I would have tried to stop you and when I couldn't, I would have gone with you."

She looked up at him, her brow arched. "You would have?"

"Of course. I'll always have your back, even if the plan is reckless."

She let out a small laugh. "Thanks."

"So this compact disc you found in Amber's closet? How are we going to see what's on it?"

"I was thinking maybe you had an old compact disc player lying around," she said hopefully.

He shook his head. "Sorry, no such luck. But I may know someone who does. James West. I can ask him."

He pulled his phone from his pocket and sent James a text. He wasn't sure if he'd get an immediate response, given the time of night, but the three little dots popped up on his screen almost as soon as he'd hit Send. Less than a minute later, he had his response.

"James says he has a compact disc player in his office at the gallery. He'll be there early tomorrow morning if we want to come by."

Karine beamed. "Perfect. Would nine tomorrow morning work for you?"

"I have to work tomorrow, but I can do nine," he said, already typing a response to James.

Karine yawned. "I'm exhausted. I'm going to go home and get some shut-eye." She turned for the door then turned back. "Hey, O. Thanks for having my back tonight."

With more conviction than he'd ever felt before in his life, he said, "Always."

THE WEST GALLERY was located in a stone-and-brick building that took up an entire Main Street block. A gold-lettered plaque was mounted on the wall next to the double glass-door entry. The interior of the gallery was two stories of bright, mostly open space.

Dozens of pieces of art were spread throughout. Some looked like traditional paintings while others seemed more like photographs, although when Omar read the descriptions next to them he learned that they, too, were paintings: hyperrealistic paintings, according to the explanations. Regardless of medium and style, they all showed extraordinary skill and talent.

James met them moments after they strode into the gallery.

"Omar. Karine. Welcome." James stepped forward and shook both their hands.

"Thanks for helping us out," Omar said.

"Not a problem. Like I said at the diner, anything I can do to help, you just need to ask. I may be the only person in town who still has a compact disc player. For work purposes, of course." James grimaced.

"Of course," Omar grinned for a moment before sobering. "We need to see what's on this." He passed the compact disc to James.

"You don't know?"

Omar shared a glance with Karine. "It may be nothing."

James's eyes danced between them before he started for the staircase leading to the second floor of the gallery, and Omar and Karine followed him, continuing the conversation. "But you don't think so."

"No," Karine said. "I think Amber was killed to stop her from showing me what is on that disc."

James's brows rose. "And how did you get this?"

"That doesn't matter," Omar said.

"I took it from Amber's house," Karine responded at the same time.

"I heard you were the one who found Amber."

"I was, but that's not when I got the CD. I went back to her house last night."

Omar shook his head.

"If he's helping us, he should know everything."

James grinned. "I appreciate the honesty. And I've hopped over the line of the law more than once. Don't worry. I'm not going to call the sheriff."

"Thanks for that," Omar deadpanned. "Shep is in charge until Lance gets back and I'm sure he wouldn't hesitate to throw us in jail."

They made a right turn at the top of the stairs into a large office space. One side of the room had large picture windows that looked out on Main Street. A cherrywood executive desk and high-backed leather chair had been placed in front of the window. On the other side of the office was another desk, this one a U-shaped computer setup complete with no less than three computer monitors and a laptop. A built-in shelf held assorted electronic equipment, including what looked like a state-of-the-art flat-screen television and a CD player.

"Okay, so let's see what we've got." James raised the hand holding the CD Omar had handed him.

He waved Omar and Karine into desk chairs in front of the computer monitors.

James slid the CD into the player and, after a moment of fuss on the television, it began to play.

It was grainy, but not so much so that they couldn't decipher that what they were looking at must've been footage from Karine's parents' home security system. It showed the front of the Eloi house.

"It looks like this must've been taken from a camera at the front of your home," Omar said, pointing to the screen. "That's your front porch and your front door, and you can even see a bit of my porch next door."

"Yeah," Karine answered in a nearly breathless whisper. "And the time and date stamp put this recording as the night my mother was killed. But I don't remember us having security cameras around the house," Karine said.

"Well, you were only twelve. It's probably something you just never thought about." Omar placed what he hoped was a soothing hand on her shoulder.

"I guess, but there must be something on here that's relevant. Why else would Amber have kept it all these years?"

The three of them continued to watch for several more minutes. A car passed the house and disappeared at the end of the street. A stray dog sauntered down the sidewalk.

"Omar, look," Karine said, pointing at a silhouetted figure that emerged from the shadows. The person was crouched down between Karine's house and his.

"There's someone there," Omar said softly.

"Can you rewind that a little?" she asked James.

James did as she asked.

They watched as the shadow moved through their yards. The person was dressed in dark colors and wore a coat with a hood pulled low over the head.

"This could be my mother's killer," she said with a shaky breath. The phone trembled in her hands.

"The video is too grainy and whoever this is, is keeping

his head down. I can't even tell if it's a man or woman," Omar said.

They watched as the person disappeared around the side of the house. They knew from the police report that the detective on the case had identified the sliding-glass door from the back porch as the entry point for the intruder. The lock had showed signs of tampering.

James fast-forwarded the video, but the person didn't enter the frame again. Whoever it was must have left the house out the back door and cut through the trees behind the house to escape. The next person to show up on the video was Jean Eloi at approximately the time the police report said he'd told the detective in charge he'd returned home.

"If you leave this with me, I'll digitize it. Maybe I can clean it up a bit and get a clearer view of the person in the shadows. If I can't do it, I'll get the tech gurus at West Investigations to take a stab at it. If they can't do it, it can't be done."

"I'd really appreciate that," Karine said "And don't worry about the costs. I'll pay whatever West Investigations' fee is."

James waved away the comment. "Let's see if it can be done first, then we can talk about the fee." He tapped a few keys on one of the keyboards on the desk and the video zoomed in on one corner of the screen.

"There was no mention of a security video in the police report about my mother's death," Karine said.

Omar frowned. "They might not have known about it." He closed his eyes, bringing up a mental picture of Karine's house. "Given the awkward angle of the shot, I'd say the camera that recorded this was tucked into the eaves around your porch."

James nodded. "That would explain why the shot is so blurry and shadowed. It's almost as if someone put the camera there but didn't want the occupants to know it. Your parents may not have even known it was there." The implication of that swirled in the air.

"But who would have done something like that?" Karine asked after a moment. "And why? Certainly not my mother's killer. He or she wouldn't want the crime on tape."

Another question to add to the growing list of questions surrounding Marilee Eloi's murder.

"You guys should look at this," James said.

Karine leaned forward in her seat. "What are we looking at?"

James pressed a few more keys and the picture cleared a little more.

"That's the Portman house," Omar said, pointing to a neighboring house on the screen. "You remember Richie and his sister, Becky, Karine? They live across the street from us."

Karine's nose scrunched in thought. "Yeah, I remember them a little. Why are we looking at their house?"

"Because I'm zoomed in on a small section of the frame that showed your intruder sneaking around your house and—" James pointed to the Portman's second-floor window "—there's someone in this window."

"That means someone may have seen the intruder," Karine stated excitedly.

"Maybe." James looked between them. "It's worth asking your neighbors about it."

Omar shook his head. "The Nelsons lived there when Karine and I were young, but they've both passed on now."

Karine's phone rang. "Thank you, James," she said, fishing her phone out of her purse and looking at the number on the screen. "I'm sorry, this is work. I have to take it."

"Feel free to use my studio. Right across the hall," James said, nodding toward the door.

Karine answered the call and strode through the door.

James leaned back in his chair, an assessing gaze trained on Omar. "Karine seems pretty determined to investigate her mother's death. Breaking into Amber Spindler's house? That was quite a risk."

"Yeah." Omar ran a hand over his short hair. "She didn't even tell me. It was lucky I saw her pulling out of her driveway. I followed her to Amber's place."

James gave him a look he couldn't read.

"What?"

"That was quite a risk for you to take too. I mean, you are a state law enforcement officer. Breaking into a private home? That could get you into some major trouble. Possibly even cost you a job I know you love."

"It wasn't much of a risk." Omar wasn't able to hold James's stare as he spoke. "I knew the house was empty. Well, except for Karine."

"Okay," James said.

Omar scowled. "What?"

"Look, I know we don't know each other very well, but from everything I've seen, you're a man with a good head on his shoulders. I know you and Karine go way back, but maybe there's more than just friendship brewing between you two."

"I…don't think so," Omar said. He wasn't sure what was going on between him and Karine, but her seeming determination to ignore their kiss didn't bode well for a budding relationship. In any event, he didn't want to discuss it with James, especially not with Karine in the next room where she might overhear.

"No? Are you sure about that?" James prodded, not taking the hint.

Karine walked back into the computer room before he could ask James what he meant. Lines of concern were etched on her forehead.

"Is everything okay?" Omar rose, crossing the floor to her.

"Yeah. Fine. Just a work thing. I took the week off, but my boss is acting like the place can't function without me. I guess I should be flattered, but it's kind of annoying too."

"Do you need to go back to Los Angeles?" Omar asked, simultaneously hoping the answer was no.

Karine shook her head. "I may have to do some work remotely this week, but I meant it when I said I wasn't leaving Carling Lake without answers. If I have to quit my job, I'll do it. Whatever it takes to finally get justice for my mother."

Omar studied the woman who'd been his friend for as long as he could remember.

She may believe that the answers were for her mother, but he knew that they were really for her. And he'd do anything for Karine, so if it was answers she needed, it was answers they'd get.

Chapter Eleven

Omar didn't have to ask Karine where their next stop was. James had made a copy of the security video for them, keeping the original for the West techs to work on enhancing. He'd also printed Karine a still photo of the person in the Portman's window.

She studied the photo silently on the drive back to their neighborhood. He drove them to his house and then they crossed the street and climbed the steps of the small concrete porch. There was no doorbell, so Omar knocked on the scarred front door.

After a long moment, the door was opened just wide enough for Richie Portman to stick his head out. "Yeah? The dogs get loose again?"

Omar had helped Richie round up his dogs more than once, but for the most part, Richie and his sister, Becky, kept to themselves.

"No, Richie," Omar said. "We're here to speak to you about something else, if you have a moment?"

Richie never seemed to have anything but moments. He and his sister had inherited the house when their mother died ten years earlier. If there was ever a father in the picture, it was before Omar's time. Becky worked at Rosie's diner part-time and Richie picked up the odd job here and there, but more often than not, he could be found at the Whiskey Wise, a dive bar on the outskirts of town.

Richie opened the door a little wider. He was only a few years older than Omar and Karine, but he looked to be a generation older. His dark brown hair had thinned so that a patch of pale white skin showed through where his hairline began. He was an inch or two taller than Omar's six foot one, but his beer gut hung over his belt and years of drinking seemed to have left his blue eyes permanently bloodshot. His fingers, rough and chapped, wrapped around a can of Bud Light.

"Who's we?" Richie scratched his chest with the hand not holding on to the beer.

"This is Karine Eloi."

Richie jerked, his eyes narrowing in on Karine. "Marilee's girl?"

"Yes. Marilee Eloi was my mother," Karine answered. "You might remember me from when my family used to live across the street."

"Kind of. I didn't pay too much attention to you two," he said, including Omar in his statement. "You were quite a bit younger than me."

Five years younger, not that much in the grand scheme of things, but Omar didn't correct him.

"What do you want to talk to me about?" Richie demanded.

Karine shifted nervously next to Omar. He squeezed her hand in support. "I have some questions for you about my mother's murder."

Richie's face registered surprise. "For me? I don't know anything about that except what I read in the papers."

"I don't think that's true, Mr. Portman," Karine shot back.

"Who all is at the door?" a woman's voice called from inside the house.

"It's the guy from across the street, Omar, and his friend Karine. Remember her?"

A hand pulled the door open wider. Becky Portman, Richie's sister, stood next to him. "What do you want?"

Karine seemed momentarily stunned by the woman's sudden appearance and abrasive demeanor. Becky was a lot to take in. Richie could be ornery, but Omar knew he was fundamentally a good guy. Becky, however, could be mean as a rattlesnake. Her bottle-red hair was teased into a bouffant that hadn't been in style since the 1950s. She was still in her uniform from the diner, but she'd accented it with large gold hoop earrings and a dozen bangles on each arm that clinked together whenever she moved.

"We were hoping to ask Richie a few questions about the night Karine's mother died."

A look passed between brother and sister. While Richie seemed to be more than a little hesitant to speak with them, Becky's lips turned down into a glower.

"I don't see how we could help, especially after all this time, but come on in then," Becky said, stepping back from the door. "You're letting the good air out, holding this door open."

The layout of the house was similar to his own, with the kitchen and dining area to the right of the entry, a long hall off to the left and the living room at the rear of the house.

Richie clomped into the kitchen and grabbed another beer from the fridge. Becky followed him and took a seat at the table. Omar and Karine followed her lead, leaving one empty chair for her brother to join them.

Richie remained standing, leaning against the short countertop next to the fridge. "What was it you wanted to ask me?"

Omar shot a look at Karine. It was her show. He was just there for moral support.

"You may have already heard that I'm looking into my mother's murder."

Becky scoffed. "Oh, we heard. It's about all anyone in town can talk about lately."

Karine cleared her throat. "I found a recording, a security video, from the night my mother was killed. And it looks like someone is standing in the window on the second floor of this house." She nodded at Richie. "I was wondering if it might have been you."

Richie shifted from one foot to the other. "How am I supposed to know? It could be. Probably is. I lived here after all. What's it to you?"

"The video is from around the time the police think my mother was killed—" Karine started.

"Hey," Richie said, pushing off the counter and waving the hand that held his beer toward the door. "If you're suggesting I had something to do with a murder, you can just get the hell out of my house right now."

Omar held up a hand while discreetly moving his chair so that Richie would have to go through him to get to Karine.

"Of course not," Karine said quickly. "If it is you in the video, that would be pretty solid proof that you weren't involved. You couldn't have been in two places at the same time."

Richie visibly calmed. "Damn straight, I wasn't involved."

"But I was thinking…well, hoping really, that you might have seen something. Maybe something you didn't even realize was important back then, but with time…"

Richie crossed his arms over his chest, his nose scrunched in thought. "I didn't see anything."

"Here." Karine pulled the still shot James had printed for her of the person in the window of the house. They'd agreed not to let on that the video showed someone skulking around the house. They didn't want to put the idea in Richie's head if he hadn't seen anything, but they also didn't know if they could trust Richie. If he had seen a person approaching the house on the night of Marilee's death, why hadn't he said anything in all these years?

"Could you look at this? Is that you?" Karine held the photo out toward Richie.

Richie made no attempt to cross the tiny kitchen and take it.

After a moment, Becky took the photo from Karine's hand. "It sure looks like it could be you. That's your bedroom window."

Richie came to stand behind his sister. "You can't tell anything from that photo. Might not even be anyone there. That could just be a shadow or some sort of glitch in your video."

"Whose shadow do you think it could be?" Omar asked, watching Richie closely. The man was too nervous. He knew something, but he'd been holding on to it for twenty-three years. He wouldn't give it up easily.

"I said it could be a shadow. Probably a glitch, like I said. All I know is it wasn't me."

"Are you sure? Could you think back to that day? Anything you remember could be of help."

"Look," Richie said, heading back to his perch next to the fridge. "I'd help you if I could. I'm sorry about your mom. She was…a nice lady."

Something about the pause Richie had taken made Omar sit up a bit straighter. He knew Karine had caught it too.

She leaned forward. "Please, if you, either of you—" Karine's eyes swept over Becky and then back to Richie "—remember anything about that night, you have to tell me."

Becky shot a look over her shoulder at her brother, then turned back to face Omar and Karine. "We don't have to do anything." She pressed her palms to the table and stood. "I think we've helped you all we can. It's time for you to go."

"Please—" Karine started.

"Let's just go, Karine," Omar said, reaching for her hand and helping her to her feet.

She shot him a glare that let him know she didn't appreciate his taking the Portmans' side. But he'd questioned enough suspects to know when to retreat and regroup. They weren't going to get anything out of either of the Portmans as long as they were together. Divide and conquer. That was the way to get the brother and sister talking. Richie was nervous enough that Omar didn't think it would take much if they distanced him from his sister. But that wasn't going to happen right now.

The front door slammed almost before they'd made it onto the little concrete porch.

"Why did you do that?" Karine stalked down the Portmans' walkway.

"Because we were getting nowhere with them," he said as they crossed the street to her house. "You aren't going to get Becky or Richie to talk if they don't want to."

"You don't know that," she growled.

"Yeah, I do." He stopped in front of her door. "This is Carling Lake, not Los Angeles. You're going to have to slow down. We can always approach Becky and Richie again. It will probably be better if we approach them separately anyway."

Karine stared at him for a long moment before letting out a huff. "Fine."

"Karine—"

"Really, Omar. I hear what you're saying. You don't have to worry about me breaking into anyone's house or doing anything rash. I plan to run some errands and see if there is anything in the house that I want to take back to Los Angeles with me."

She stepped inside her house and closed the door, leaving him standing on the porch alone.

Chapter Twelve

Karine knew she'd been a little snappish with Omar, but his suggestion that she slow down had irked her. Her mother's killer had been walking free, maybe in Carling Lake, for twenty-three years. She only had a week to find answers or to at least jump-start the sheriff's reinvestigation. And although she had more than enough banked vacation to extend her stay, she knew it would be a tough sell getting her boss to sign off on any additional time.

That meant slowing down just wasn't an option. But she had told Omar the truth about what she'd planned to do that day. She still needed to buy as many mousetraps as she could find and set them out in the attic. After a thorough consultation with the clerk at the hardware store, she returned home with traps designed to drive the little critters away.

She climbed the stairs leading to the attic and, with a bit of force, was able to push the warped door open inch by inch until there was a space big enough for them to slip through.

Karine froze, shocked. She knew her mother had used the space as a studio when she was alive, but she'd expected it to have been emptied out like the rest of the house when she and her father had moved out. Apparently, her dad had forgotten to instruct the movers to pack up the attic when they'd packed up the rest of the house.

She felt a shiver run down her back. Hesitant now to move too far past the doorway, she slowly turned in a circle, taking in the room. The sloped ceiling gave the space a small, cramped feeling in spite of the window opening out on a view of the Carling Lake Forest, a small section of the lake and the mountains. The view, Karine remembered, that had compelled her mother to turn the attic into her studio in the first place.

Stepping into the space felt like stepping back in time. Her mother's art studio hadn't been touched in twenty-three years. A half-finished canvas depicting a gloomy, almost macabre woodland scene sat on an easel. Next to it was a table with long-dried paints, stiffened paintbrushes and an empty mason jar. Several of her mother's paintings—some finished, some not—leaned against the wall, along with a stack of empty canvases. Her mother's smock hung on the wall hook next to the door. Everything was covered in several layers of dust and dirt. She felt a pang of loss for her mother and what could have been—her mother's potential.

"It's like stepping back in time," she murmured.

She ventured farther into the space, imagining her mother standing in front of her easel, assessing the unfinished canvas. Although the subject of her paintings was always nature, the mood Marilee Eloi had been able to convey was different with each one. The painting in front of Karine was clearly taking a darker tone. Leaning in close, she could see a woman in the thick of the trees, almost hidden. She appeared to be running, looking back over her shoulder with an expression of terror on her face, as if she were being chased by something, or someone, terrifying.

She couldn't help but wonder if that was a reflection of her mother's frame of mind in the days and weeks prior to her murder. Did Marilee suspect that she might be in danger? Could her last paintings somehow point them to her killer?

It was almost like her mother was there in the room with her, like she'd just stepped away for a moment, but planned to be right back.

But, of course, Karine knew that wasn't the case. Her mother would never hold her again and she wouldn't ever finish the painting on the easel or step foot in her studio again.

Karine couldn't get lost in grief. It was only natural that everything she'd been through in the last few days—being back in Carling Lake, getting shot at, the email from Amber and then her overdose—would dredge up a myriad of feelings, but she had to focus. Something in this attic might point her toward her mother's killer.

She took one more look back at the painting on the easel. Her mother had been really talented.

Too bad she hadn't gotten a lick of her mother's talent. Or her father's passion for plants. She'd gone out on a limb of her own with her interest in numbers and finance. Or really not gone out on a limb. Finance was safe. Steady. She was sure a therapist would have a field day exploring the connection between having lost her mother as a child and her desire for dependability.

She turned away from the easel. In addition to her mother's painting stuff, there was a large chest with four drawers on each side of a middle panel. A golden tree was painted on the panel, its branches reaching out and extending onto each of the drawers.

She remembered then how she'd loved that chest. Her mother hadn't let her into the attic very often. She hadn't wanted her making a mess or destroying her paintings, but Karine had loved this golden tree. When she was little, her mother would take her on long walks in the woods behind the house and they'd search for golden trees. Of course, they'd never found one, but it was the journey, not the destination, that she'd treasured.

The scavenger hunts had come to an end after Karine had asked her dad if he could help her research golden trees and where she could find one. He'd told her that there was no such thing. Then her parents had gotten into an argument. Her dad thought her mother shouldn't have been misleading her about science. Her mother had countered that the walks fostered creativity and that maybe if someone had done the same for him, he wouldn't be so dull.

The memory came pouring back into her head as if it had happened yesterday. Along with other memories of her parents fighting. Her parents had quarreled a lot, she realized. How could she have forgotten that? But coming back to this house, stepping into the attic, seemed to have opened up a well of memories she'd locked away deep in her head.

Her parents hadn't really talked to each other as much as they'd argued with each other. She'd always remembered their family Friday night movie dates, as her mother had called them, for the quintessential family time, but now she tried to remember if they had ever talked to one another or looked at each other during those nights. With hindsight, it was almost as if they'd been going through the motions of what they'd thought they should be doing to be a family. They'd always made her sit between them and she'd thought it was because she liked to be in charge of the popcorn bowl, but now she wondered if it had been more to put as much distance as they could between themselves.

Karine shuddered out a deep breath as her memories seemed to twist and rotate to form a picture that was very different from what she'd always thought about her childhood.

She opened the drawers in the chest. The only things inside the first seven drawers were massive dust bunnies. But in the bottom right drawer, she found a plastic mood ring.

She gasped, reaching inside and drawing it out. Her old mood ring.

She held the ring out and inspected it. She'd loved that ring. Her father had won it for her at the Carling Lake fair when she was eight. She'd worn it every day for nearly a year. She'd totally forgotten about it.

She slid the ring onto her ring finger, back where it belonged.

Then she remembered something else about this chest of drawers. There was a secret compartment in the middle panel. It was part of the reason she'd liked the piece so much.

The release lever was in one of the corners, she was pretty sure. She pressed on the upper left corner, but nothing happened. She moved to the upper right corner, but still the panel didn't open.

"Could be rusted shut," she said out loud to herself.

Then, in a flash, she remembered. She pressed both corners at the same time, and the panel slid out. "Got it."

There wasn't space to hide much of anything, but her mother had stuck a thin notebook between the slats of the drawer.

Karine plucked it free and wiped the layer of dust clinging to the cover from it. She ran her hand over the gilded gold words on the front. She opened it, immediately recognizing her mother's looping cursive letters. Her mother's diary.

Based on the dates at the beginning of each entry, her mother had started writing in the diary about a year before her murder. The last entry was dated two weeks prior to Marilee's death.

"This is it. If my mother suspected she was in any danger, she'd have written it in here." She skimmed through the pages of the books. Nothing in it suggested her mother had been having issues with anyone.

A piece of yellowed paper fluttered from between the last pages of the diary.

Karine knelt. Opening the folded paper and reading, she rose. Her knees began to shake as she read.

The love letter trembled in her hand.

Her mother had been having an affair.

Chapter Thirteen

Karine hadn't known what to expect when she'd searched her mother's studio, but she certainly hadn't expected to find evidence that her mother had been having an affair. This must be what the note in the police report about "affair" had meant. Her mother had been having an affair. Who was her lover? And how long had it gone on? Had Marilee still been involved with the man when she died? Could her lover be her killer?

She flipped through the diary, reading as fast as she could, looking for the name of her mother's lover. There was nothing to even suggest whom Marilee may have had an affair with. Mostly, the diary detailed Marilee's hopes for her artist career. There were some references to Karine, and one or two about her father, but the diary was pretty benign. Boring even.

The question swirled in her head. Omar had warned her that she'd probably have to talk to her father, get him to open up, if she really hoped to find answers about her mother's death, and it seemed he was right.

She had to tell her father about the affair.

Six months ago she would have said that her father was going to be devastated by the news, but now, with her memories so jumbled, leaving her unsure of what parts of her childhood were real and what parts she'd glossed over, she wasn't so sure. Regardless of how her father reacted, he deserved to know the truth about his marriage, and she wouldn't have felt right keeping such a big secret from him.

Karine left the mousetraps in the attic and took a second shower. While she got dressed in jeans and a light sweater, she took the time to consider, then reject, the idea of asking Omar to drive with her to Connecticut.

It wasn't that she wouldn't have liked the company. She was finding that she more than liked being in the company of Omar, a feeling she was starting to believe she'd have to give some serious thought to at some point. But not now. She was about to spring some potentially upsetting news on her father, and she didn't want it to be any more uncomfortable than it had to be.

She shot Omar a quick text, telling him she was going to visit her father and would be back that evening, before leaving for Springtree. The bright sunny day was a contrast with the heavy feeling sitting in the pit of her stomach as she made the drive.

The afternoon traffic was light, and she made it to her father's brick ranch-style home just after three in the afternoon, having only made one pit stop for a quick lunch. The tall oak in the front yard still stretched up to the sky and the flower beds lining the front walk had been freshly mulched.

Her father had always taken great pride in the yard, no surprise, given his chosen career as a botanist. When she turned into the asphalt driveway and parked behind the sky blue Subaru station wagon, she also wasn't surprised to find her father in the yard, pushing the lightweight battery-operated mower she'd gotten him last Father's Day.

Jean Eloi had grown pudgy as he'd aged. Her stepmother's rich cooking hadn't done anything to help him keep the weight off. His gray hair was cut short all around, and his face was lined with its fair share of wrinkles. She smiled, taking in his attire. Khakis, a blue-and-white-checked, short-sleeved dress shirt and brilliantly white sneakers. He looked like the college professor he was even when doing yard work. That was her dad.

A smile bloomed on her father's face, and he stepped from behind the mower as she got out of the car.

"Well, this is a welcome surprise. I was wondering when you were going to get around to visiting your old man."

She let her father pull her into a warm hug. "I've only been on the east coast for a few days, and you are not old."

"Old enough that two days can seem like a lifetime when I haven't seen my beautiful daughter."

"Dad." She rested her head on his shoulder for a brief moment.

"Come on. Stephanie made fresh lemonade and I could use a cold drink."

Her father and Stephanie had married a year after her mother's death. Stephanie had tried to form a close, motherly bond, but Karine had been thirteen by then and the combination of having lost her mother and teenage hormones had made it difficult going.

In the years since she'd moved out of the house, her relationship with Stephanie had gotten better. They were not only cordial, but friendly most of the time. No doubt the three-thousand-plus miles that usually separated them had played a big role in mellowing the relationship.

It wasn't that she disliked Stephanie, her stepmother clearly made her father happy, and she was a nice enough woman. She'd done her best to be someone Karine could count on as she'd moved from teenhood into womanhood, but no matter what Stephanie did, she'd never be Marilee. She knew it wasn't fair to compare Stephanie to her mother, but fair or not, Karine couldn't help it. Deep down inside her, there would always be a little girl wishing it was her mother standing next to her father.

"Look who's here!" her father proclaimed loudly as they stepped into the kitchen.

Stephanie was at the stove. She looked up, blinking as if she wasn't sure of what she was seeing. "Karine. This is a surprise. A wonderful surprise, that is."

Karine had told her father of her plans to go to Carling Lake, although she'd left out the portion where she'd planned to look into her mother's death. All she'd told her father was that she'd wanted to get a good look at the house she now owned and make some decisions. She had no idea how much, if anything, Jean had relayed to Stephanie. It was quite possible her showing up like this was a total surprise to her stepmom. Her father could be a bit of an absentminded professor. Or an absentminded semiretired professor, now that he was only teaching one class per semester.

Stephanie wiped her hands on the apron she was wearing then stepped around the island stove to give Karine a brief hug.

"Hi, Stephanie. I hope my dropping in isn't a problem.

Dad did tell you I was going to be in Carling Lake for a few weeks, right?"

Stephanie waved a hand. "Of course it's not a problem. This will always be your home. And yes, your dad remembered to tell me that you were going to be in our neck of the woods for a while." Stephanie sent an adoring smile her husband's way. "I'm so glad you found the time to visit."

Karine thought she heard the slight edge in the last sentence. It had been a while since she'd last made it to the east coast. Her father didn't like to fly, so his and Stephanie's visits to the west coast were few and far between. That left them video calling one another every few weeks, calls that they mostly kept to talking about work, weather and Springtree gossip even though Karine didn't really know many of the residents anymore. Nothing too personal or revealing about their lives. Sometimes Karine wished she and her father, and even she and Stephanie, had a closer relationship, and she got the feeling her father and Stephanie felt the same way, but none of them seemed to know how to forge that kind of relationship with each other.

Karine hopped up onto a stool to the side of the island while Stephanie took her place behind the stove again. It looked like she was making a sauce of some kind. It smelled delicious, like basil and garlic and something sweet she didn't have the culinary chops to name. One thing Karine had to hand to Stephanie, she was one hell of a cook. "I wanted to take a couple of days to get settled in Carling Lake before I dropped in on you."

"Yes, and how is the house?" Stephanie asked, stirring the pot.

Her father poured lemonade into two glasses and handed one of the glasses to Karine.

"It's fine. Better than I expected, actually. The trustee has been taking good care of it." Karine took a sip of lemonade.

"You'll probably get a pretty penny for it," her father said around a sip of lemonade. "Carling Lake has exploded as a vacation destination in recent years. You might even be able to start a bidding war. I know a couple of good Realtors."

"Maybe." Karine took another swallow from her glass.

Stephanie's sharp gaze landed on Karine, but her father kept talking.

"Now is a good time to sell too. Have you seen the way the real estate market is surging? You'd think after the calamity in twenty-o-eight people would be more cautious, but we never seem to learn." Her father shook his head. "Ah, well, it could be good for you though," her father continued, oblivious to her hesitation about selling.

"You do plan to sell the house, right?" Stephanie asked, still stirring the sauce slowly, her eyes trained on Karine.

Now Karine remembered something else that had vexed her about Stephanie when she'd been a teen. She could never get anything by her. If it had just been her father, she could have stayed out all night every night and Jean wouldn't have noticed. But Stephanie… Karine had often wondered if Stephanie had been a wild adolescent. She'd seemed to instinctively know what youthful shenanigans Karine was planning to get into and was always ready to head her off at the pass. She knew she should probably be grateful to her stepmother for that, but right now the old teenage irritation was back.

"I'm not sure what I want to do," Karine answered.

Her father's body jerked. "What do you mean you aren't sure? I thought you came back to the east coast to settle everything. Sell the property. Close out the trust."

"I did come to settle some things, but that doesn't mean I plan to sell the house."

"What does it mean?" Stephanie stopped stirring. "Are you thinking about moving back to Carling Lake?"

Karine felt herself revolt at the idea. New York winters, no way. She might have been born on the east coast, but she was a west coast girl through and through.

"I don't think that's in the cards." She couldn't be sure, but she thought she saw Stephanie's shoulders sag in relief.

"What does it mean?" her father pressed.

"I don't know exactly. I'm still figuring that out. Actually, I wanted to talk to you about some things." She cleared her throat, unsure how to say she wanted to talk to her father in private without offending Stephanie. It was her house, after all. "It's a little sensitive. No offense to you, Stephanie."

"No, no." Stephanie gave her a strained smile. "I understand there are things you and your father need to speak about. You two go ahead to your father's den. Karine, you do plan to stay for dinner, yes? I'm making sweet Italian sausages smothered in my famous tomato basil sauce."

Karine's stomach grumbled in anticipation. She gave her stepmother a genuine smile. "I wouldn't miss it."

Stephanie returned the smile before Karine turned and followed her father down the short hallway to the fourth bedroom that they'd taken to referring to as his den.

Her father sat in the leather executive chair at his desk,

turning it to face the ratty old recliner that Stephanie had been fighting to get him to throw out for years. On one of their most recent video calls, her father had lamented that Stephanie had finally put her foot down and insisted that if he was going to keep the recliner, he had to move it into his den where she couldn't see it.

"Compromise is the key to a happy marriage," her father had told her, admitting the recliner had found a new home in the den.

It seemed that her father had taken the opportunity to freshen up his office too. The walls were still lined with the same photos of various flora and fauna, like they'd always been, but the dingy orange paint had been changed to more updated and neutral grayish-blue and the dark wood built-in bookshelves had been painted a fresh, crisp white.

"So," her father said after they'd both taken a seat, "what did you want to talk to me about?"

"I wanted to ask you some questions," she started hesitantly.

Her father's expression was curious but still open, which she took as a good sign. "Sure. Shoot."

It wasn't an easy topic to bring up. *Did you know that your wife, my mother, was having an affair before she was murdered?* Not something that a daughter usually had to discuss with her father. There was no YouTube video detailing the five steps for easing into the conversation.

"I was in Mom's studio earlier today and I found something."

Her father's brow furrowed. "Studio? You mean the attic?"

"Yes. You know Mom had it set up as a studio. There were several paintings still up there, one that she must have been working on when she was killed. It looked like it hadn't been touched since the day she died."

The lines in her father's face deepened. "I didn't know that. I paid a moving company to pack up our things. I couldn't bring myself to go back into the house after your mother's untimely passing."

Karine didn't think she'd ever heard her father refer to her mother's death as what it was. A murder. Or even that she'd been killed. He'd always referred to it as "her untimely passing."

And that had always irritated her.

Her mother hadn't just passed away. It hadn't been an act of God or even an accident. Someone had purposely taken Marilee Eloi's life. Someone who had never been brought to justice.

She tamped down on her irritation. "Well, I guess they didn't think to look in the attic, because I don't think anyone has been up there in more than twenty years. The door was locked, so I guess someone might have been, but nothing had been touched."

"Okay. Well, it shouldn't be too much trouble to clear the space out," her father said. "I'm sure you'd like to have the paintings that are there, but most of the stuff is probably trash, right?"

Karine nodded. "A lot of it can be thrown out and, yes, I'd love to have my mother's paintings." She already had several hanging on the walls in her condo. Her father had had the foresight to keep and store the paintings that had been on the walls in their home when her mother died. When she'd bought her condo in Los Angeles, she'd had them shipped to the west coast.

"But I also discovered a chest of drawers in the studio." She waited to see if the chest rang any bells with her father. His blank look told her it did not. "I guess you don't remember it—"

"I rarely went into the attic," her father conceded.

"I remembered that this chest had a special feature. A kind of secret drawer in the middle panel. When I opened it, I found Mom's diary." She reached into her purse and pulled out the diary. She handed it to her father.

A small smile sent the ends of his mouth upward. "I'd forgotten that Marilee wrote in a diary."

"So, it's hers."

"If it was in the attic, it had to be your mother's. Marilee had been writing in a diary since before we met. She had dozens packed away spanning years."

"There are more diaries?" She was surprised. She didn't remember her mother ever writing in a diary, but perhaps it was something she hadn't done in front of her young daughter.

Her father shrugged. "Sure. If you don't have them already, they are probably in a box in the basement or in my storage locker."

"Could you get them for me?"

"Of course. As far as I'm concerned, all of your mother's things belong to you now. It may take me a few days though."

"That's fine. Um… I didn't just find the diary."

Her father tilted his head, curiosity in his eyes. "No? What else did you find?"

She inhaled deeply. "There's no easy way to say this, but I found a love letter."

"A love letter?" Jean looked thoughtful. "I don't remember your mother and I ever exchanging love letters."

Karine pulled the letter from her purse. "I don't think the letter is from you. Dad, I think Mom was having an affair."

Her father studied her for a long second then laughed. "Honey, you must be mistaken."

"No, Dad. I don't think I am." She handed him the letter. "I found this in Mom's diary. I know it's not dated or signed, but it's pretty explicitly a love letter and it's pretty clear that Mom was having an affair with whoever wrote this."

Her father's face lost its color as he read the note. She felt sick. He didn't deserve this betrayal by his wife. For the first time in as long as she could remember, Karine was angry at her mother.

"Dad, I know this is a shock, but if Mom was having an affair, that could open up a whole new line of investigation regarding her murder. I mean, maybe she tried to break it off and her lover became enraged. Maybe he wanted her to leave you, us, and she wouldn't. Maybe—"

"Karine, stop!" Her father looked up, his eyes flashing with something she couldn't name.

"Dad?"

"This letter, it wasn't written to your mother."

She blinked, baffled. "But I found it in her diary."

"I don't know how your mother got her hands on it. She must have suspected and gone snooping in my things."

A nauseous feeling built in her stomach. "Snooping? Dad—"

Embarrassment seeded her father's expression. "Karine, your mother wasn't the one having an affair. I was. The letter is mine."

Chapter Fourteen

Karine couldn't move.

Her father had had an affair. He'd cheated on her mother.

Her skin prickled. "But the letter…it was in Mom's diary."

"She must have found it." He handed the piece of yellowed paper back to her. "I never realized it was missing."

She gripped the letter until her knuckles turned white. "She never confronted you?"

Her father shook his head, looking more than a little green around the gills. "She never said a word. I never even suspected."

She shook. A buzz grew in her ears. She'd fainted once before and knew she was close to repeating the experience again. She leaned forward, putting her head between her legs, gripping the arms of the chair.

"Honey, it was a long time ago. Your mother and I were having difficulties—"

Karine held up a hand, imploring her father to stop speaking. She felt like she was on the precipice of falling over a cliff. One more word and over she'd go.

Her father stopped talking. They sat in silence for several minutes.

When the buzz in her ears finally receded, she asked, "How long?"

"What?"

She sat up and looked into her father's eyes. "How long did the affair go on? When did it start? Was it still going on when Mom—" She couldn't bring herself to directly ask what she really wanted to know. Was he still with this other woman when her mother was murdered?

Her father's cheeks flushed and his gaze skittered away. "I don't think—"

"I don't care what you think. How long were you cheating on Mom?"

He sighed. "You have to understand, sweetheart—"

"Don't call me that."

Her father's back stiffened. He blinked and then his face took on an expression of resolve. "Okay, okay." He let out a breath. "It wasn't just an affair. It was a relationship. Your mother and I had been in a bad place for a long time. I didn't know she knew about the affair, but I was planning on asking her for a divorce. She was killed before I worked up the nerve."

"A relationship?" Even though she'd asked him for the details, she was struggling to make sense of them. And then it suddenly made all the sense in the world.

Karine glanced at the closed office door, bile rising in her throat. Her father and Stephanie had married a little more than a year after her mother had been killed. She'd always assumed the marriage had happened so fast because her father had wanted her to have a female role model in her life. A mother figure. But that hadn't been the reason at all.

"Oh, my—" Karine pressed a hand against her stomach, willing the bile in her throat to stay down. Her father had been having an affair with Stephanie. All this time, he'd been married to the woman he'd cheated on her mother with.

"Honey." He reached out a hand.

She leaned away from his touch.

Her father sat back. "Karine, all of this happened a long time ago. It has nothing to do with our lives now."

Karine glared at her father. "It may have been a long time ago for you, but it's happening right now for me." She shot to her feet. "I have to go."

"Karine—" Her father stood, but she was already through the office door.

Stephanie called out as she slammed out of the house, but she didn't look back.

Her entire body trembled, her hands shaking so violently that she dropped the car keys on the front walkway. She scooped them up and turned toward her car.

Omar.

He leaned against the rental, his legs crossed at the ankles, his arms crossed over his chest.

The dam of tears she'd been holding back broke at the sight of him.

He was at her side in a millisecond, wrapping her in his arms. "What's wrong? What happened?"

It was too much. It was all just too much. "Get me out of here. Please."

"You got it." Omar led her to his truck, helping her hop up into the passenger seat before jogging around to the driver's side. He started the engine and headed away from her father's house.

She wasn't sure how long they'd been driving when she finally got a hold of the emotions swamping her.

"Feel better?" Omar said once the deluge had ceased.

"A little."

"Want to talk about it?"

She nodded. "Could we go somewhere else though? I need to get away from here, but I don't trust myself to drive yet."

"Okay then. There's something I want to show you."

THEY WERE HEADED away from Karine's father's house, but in the opposite direction from Carling Lake. Omar didn't push her to tell him what had happened at her father's house. Whatever it was he could tell it had gotten to her.

"My father cheated on my mother," she said after they'd been on the road for a little while. Once she'd started talking the events of the day spilled out of her. How she'd found a love letter in her mother's things in the attic and had believed her mother had been having an affair when she'd been killed. Then going to her father and finding out that the letter had belonged to him.

He hadn't seen that coming. "Wow. How do you feel about that?"

Karine stared out of the front windshield. "I don't want to talk about it."

"Understood."

They drove in silence for twenty more minutes before Omar pulled off the main highway. He turned them onto a dusty little side road that looked like it hadn't been used in decades. A few minutes later, he turned into what had once been a popular drive-in movie theater.

"Where are we?"

"The former Stardust & Moonlight Drive-in Theater."

The screen had tears in several places, but it still stood like a sentry over the cracked parking lot. He backed the pickup in so the truck's bed faced the screen.

Karine quirked an eyebrow. "I don't think they're showing a movie tonight. Or ever again."

He chuckled. "No. This place closed in 2006."

"Sooooo, what are we doing here?"

He pointed at the windshield. "Looking at a different kind of stars. Come on."

The sky had already started to darken, and the stars peeked through what was left of the waning daylight.

He grabbed a blanket, a couple of power bars and two bottles of water from the go-bag he kept in the back seat of the pickup and got out.

He hopped into the truck bed and spread out the blanket before helping Karine into the back of the truck.

They sat in comfortable silence for a while. The stars had not only come out, they'd brought a full moon with them. It all gleamed brilliantly against the inky midnight sky.

"How did you even know about this place?"

"This is embarrassing. After you moved to Springtree, I learned everything I could about this place. I know there used to be a Mister Softee downtown and your violin teacher taught out of her house on Munkhouser Road, and that trash pickup was on Tuesdays in your zip code."

He waited a beat, fearing he'd said too much. In his twelve-year-old mind, knowing everything about the town where she'd moved had made him feel closer to her, but out loud now, he wondered if she'd think he was a preteen stalker.

She chuckled. "Wow, you really got to know this town."

"I missed you," he said.

"I missed you too." She reached for his hand.

They leaned back against the pickup's cab and stared out at the stars. The air was crisp, but it was a welcome coolness.

"I used to imagine bringing you here one day to watch one of those terrible sci-fi movies you love." The words he'd been wanting to say for…for years now, bubbled up inside him.

Just say it... I want to be more than just your best friend. I want to be your man.

I love you, Karine.

"*Barbarella* is a classic, and I will fight anyone who says otherwise."

He grinned. "I don't want to fight." Fighting was the last thing he had on his mind at the moment. Quite the opposite, actually. "I had a huge crush on you when we were teens."

She turned toward him, focusing her eyes on him. The moonlight created flecks like fireworks exploding in her light brown eyes. "You did?"

His heart pounded as if he'd just come back from a ten-mile run. "I did." He squeezed her hand.

She squeezed back. "I had a crush on you too," she said quietly, a shadow of a smile passing over her face.

He held her gaze. They were headed for potentially dangerous waters. Heaven knew he wanted to kiss her so badly right now that he could almost taste her lips on his.

As he searched her eyes, he was sure she felt the same way.

He let go of her hand and lifted his to cradle the sides

of her face, angling her head up as he tilted down. He hovered for a moment, their mouths millimeters apart, savoring the moment.

He skimmed his lips across hers, drawing a small hum of pleasure from her throat that went right to his groin.

Karine reached out, her hands going to his waist, drawing him closer. The encouragement emboldened him and he coaxed her mouth open, deepening the kiss, their tongues tangling, dancing an exquisite dance. Desire pulsated in a current between them.

Karine moved her hands up, curling her fingers around his neck. He moved his hands down her back, cupping her bottom.

She sighed into his mouth then threw one of her legs over his so that she was straddling him.

He nearly came undone. He couldn't remember the last time he'd been this turned on by just making out. But then, Karine could turn him on with a look.

He scraped along the side of her breast. His body was begging him for more, and from the way Karine was grinding against him, she was right there with him.

The blast of an eighteen-wheeler's horn from the nearby highway shook the pickup.

They were too far away for anyone to have seen their hot and heavy make-out session from the road, but the blast of sound had an immediate chilling effect on the mood.

Karine swung off him, pushing her back into the side of the truck and putting as much distance as was possible in the limited space they had between them. "I…" She pressed a hand to her lips, swollen by his kisses. "I think you should take me back to my father's place to pick up my car."

She hurried to get out of the truck bed and around to the passenger's-side door. She was already strapped into her seat belt by the time he hauled himself behind the wheel.

"Karine, I'm sorry if—"

She held up a hand, her eyes flicking to his before skittering away. "Don't be sorry. I'm not, really. We just got carried away. It happens. No big deal."

No big deal.

He swallowed down the pain that arose with those words and started the truck.

No big deal. It felt like a big deal. A huge, life-altering deal.

Chapter Fifteen

It was just after nine in the evening when Omar pulled into his driveway just as his cell phone began to ring.

James.

He answered the call and exited the truck, watching across the expanse that separated his house from Karine's as she got out of her rental car.

"Omar? Are you there?" James's voice sounded through the phone.

He realized he'd answered the call, but hadn't yet spoken.

"I'm here. Sorry. What's up?"

"I wanted to make sure you and Karine heard about Becky Portman."

He spun to look at the Portman house across the street. It was dark. It didn't appear that anyone was at home. "What about Becky?"

"She was attacked earlier today. From what I've gathered, she got home from work and she must have surprised a burglar," James said.

Karine must have clocked the concern on his face. She walked across their lawns and stopped next to him on the driver's side of the pickup truck. "What's going on?"

"Becky Portman was attacked in her house earlier today. James says it looks like a burglary gone wrong."

"Becky was taken to the hospital. Richie found her, and she'd been hit on the head pretty hard. No updates on her condition yet."

Omar repeated what James said to Karine. His heart tightened at the stricken look on her face. Becky and Richie Portman were far from the nicest people, but he and Karine had known them both for most of their lives. They were fixtures in the neighborhood and in the Carling Lake community.

"I'm going to keep my ear to the ground," James continued, "but I wanted to make sure you'd heard the news. I'm sure you're keeping your eyes open, but with everything going on and you and Karine living right across the street…" He let the rest of the sentence fall away.

James didn't need to finish. A burglary at the Portman house hit more than a little close to home. Especially given everything else that had happened in the last few days and the fact that they'd just spoken to Becky and Richie about the night Karine's mother was murdered. Burglaries in Carling Lake happened, although they weren't common, and bad actors tended to target the tourists more than the residents. A sick feeling was growing in the pit of his stomach. The timing of this burglary did not feel coincidental.

He signed off the call.

"I'm going to go to the hospital," Karine said. "I'm sure Richie is there and whatever my issues with him and Becky, they are all each other has. I'm sure he could use some support."

Omar smiled, ever surprised by her kindness. "I'll drive."

Karine rounded the pickup and hopped in.

They rode in silence for several minutes before Karine spoke.

"Do you think…?"

"Do I think that a burglary at the Portman place is a little too coincidental, given we just confronted them about the possibility that they'd seen something on the night of your mother's death? Yes, the thought had crossed my mind."

Karine chewed her bottom lip. "But that would mean the attack on Becky was our fault."

"No," he said definitively. "It does not. The attack on Becky is the fault of whoever attacked her. No one else."

His glance across the cab told him his words hadn't convinced her.

The parking lot at the hospital wasn't crowded. Neither was the waiting room. Richie was the only person there. He sat, hunched over in a waiting room chair, with his head in his hands.

"Richie," Omar said.

Richie looked up with a mixture of hope and despair on his face. "Oh, it's only you two."

Omar let the comment roll off him.

"How is Becky?" Karine asked, taking the seat next to Richie. "How are you?"

Omar sat in the plastic chair on Richie's other side.

Richie scraped a hand over his face. It was pretty clear he wasn't doing well. He had a five-o'clock shadow and his eyes were bloodshot from crying. "The doctors haven't told me anything."

"Have you talked to the police?" Omar asked.

"Deputy Coben was just here, checking in on me and Becky, and Deputy Bridges took my statement while the

EMTs got Becky ready to transport. I don't know much though. I came home and found her in the back room. She was lying on the floor..." He choked up. "There was so much blood. I called 9-1-1. That's it." Richie let his head fall into his hands again.

Karine rubbed his back soothingly. "Hey, Becky is tough. She's going to come through this."

"Deputy Coben said it looked like a robbery." Richie lifted his head. Tears showed in his eyes. He shook his head. "It wasn't a robbery. Becky, she regained consciousness for a minute while we were waiting for the ambulance to arrive."

Omar and Karine shared a look across Richie's back. "Did she say who attacked her?"

Richie shook his head. "No. She didn't say who attacked her, but she did say something."

The tense moment swirled around them.

Richie turned to look at Karine. "She said, 'Tell Karine she's in danger.'"

THE KILLER THREW the glass in his hand across the room. Becky Portman wasn't dead and Karine knew about the security recording of the night of Marilee's murder. A video that she had and was no doubt studying to find out who was on it. They could do amazing things with old videos nowadays.

A terrified shiver snaked through him.

The time for warnings was over.

He had to get the video and eliminate the threat posed by Karine. Her boyfriend would be a problem, so he'd have to go too.

Chapter Sixteen

Karine was relieved when she woke up the next day to a text from Daton Spindler, Amber's ex-husband, agreeing to meet her for coffee that morning. Her make-out session with Omar had supercharged the feelings she hadn't known were there for him. And now she didn't seem able to tame them. Her dreams had been filled with him. Kissing him. Touching him. Making love to him. She wasn't sure what to do with that, so she planned to ignore it for now. She had enough on her plate anyway.

She lucked out and found a space right in front of OrganicSandwich. The interior was trendy for Carling Lake but had a homey feel. A soft, jazzy song wafted from the overhead speakers and the entire shop smelled like freshly baked bread. She closed her eyes and inhaled the delicious aroma.

Daton was already at the café when Karine arrived. He stood as she approached the table and engulfed her in a fatherly hug.

He gestured to the cups of steaming coffee already on the café table. "I ordered both of us regular coffees because I wasn't sure what you wanted to drink. I don't have a lot of time before I have to get into the office. But I was so thrilled to get your text asking if we could meet up this morning."

She didn't tell him she didn't drink coffee. She'd texted him the night before after getting home. She'd gotten so much new information over the last twenty-four or so hours about her parents, and she wasn't sure anymore if she could trust her father. There weren't a lot of other people who could help her make sense of what had been happening around the time her mother was killed. Daton was one of the few.

"You look so much like your mother," he said, taking the seat on the opposite side of the table from her.

"Really? You think so?"

He seemed surprised. "You don't?"

"I don't really know. I haven't seen a lot of pictures of my mother. I used to think my dad didn't keep them around because seeing her was too hard for him."

"But you don't think that's the reason anymore?"

"I don't know what to think right now." She swallowed hard, pushing down the emotion swelling in her chest. "I found out some things about my father and my mother. Things about their relationship around the time of her murder."

Daton looked at her with an expression of confusion. "What things are you talking about?"

"That my father was having an affair. My mother knew."

Confusion morphed into surprise on Daton's face. "Whoa, whoa, wait a minute. Marilee, Amber and I were pretty close back then. Marilee never said a word about Jean straying."

"He did." She ran a finger around the rim of the cup of

coffee she wasn't drinking. "He admitted it to me after I found a love letter in my mother's diary. At first I thought it was to her. That my mother was the one who'd had an affair."

Daton shook his head vehemently. "No, Marilee had far too much integrity to treat a family like that."

"Well, apparently my father didn't," she snapped.

"I can't believe this. Your mother never said a word. I guess you never really know what goes on inside a marriage."

His comment reminded her that he had at one time been married to Amber. "I'm sorry. I'm bringing up all this stuff and I haven't even said I'm sorry for your loss."

He waved away the comment. "Thank you, but Amber and I haven't had any kind of relationship since the divorce more than three years ago now. To be honest with you, my comment about marriage was more about my first marriage than anything you've told me about your parents. It's no big secret in this town that my marriage to Amber ended when she found out I'd been having an affair with Valerie, my current wife."

It may have been common knowledge to the residents of Carling Lake, but it was news to Karine. She wasn't sure how to respond to it and, frankly, she wasn't feeling very forgiving toward cheaters at the moment, so she decided to move on.

"Can you tell me anything about my mother in the weeks and months before her death that might help me figure out why she was killed?"

Daton gave her a look that was half pity, half sadness. "Nothing. I'm sorry, but I've thought about that time, those weeks and days before and after Marilee's murder now. There was nothing unusual going on that I knew about before your mother was killed and I've had to come to the conclusion that it was just one of those tragic, horrible things that happens in life."

She couldn't accept that. "So you think the police are right? That my mother interrupted a burglar and was killed?"

"After so much time and no new evidence, no one speaking up, yes, I think the only logical conclusion is that someone, probably a tourist or one of the seasonal workers, thought the house was empty and was surprised by your mother." He reached across the table and took her hand. "I do know that Marilee wouldn't want you to spend your life consumed by her death. She would want you to move on. Fall in love. Start a family and give her grandbabies to look down on from heaven."

A mental picture of Omar popped into her head, but she shook it away. She didn't know if marriage, family and babies were in her future, but if they were, it was in the distant future. Right now, she had to find closure for her past before she could move forward. But she could tell from the look on Daton's face that he didn't want to hear that. Like a lot of people after a tragedy, he just wanted to move on. Get back to normal. But they never understood that life had not been normal for her since she'd been twelve years old. And it never would be.

Daton twisted his wrist to look at the Rolex watch on it. "I'm sorry, but I have an early meeting today. I have to go, but maybe we could get together again? Dinner at my house, maybe. I have tons of old pictures of your mother,

Amber and I when we were younger. I can dig them out of my attic and you can take a look at them."

She gave him a genuine smile. She'd loved to get a glimpse into her mother's childhood. "I'd love that. Thank you."

She stood, and Daton gave her another hug. "I'll call you soon to set something up."

Karine watched him walk out of the café with the stride of a man who knew his place in the world.

She would definitely look forward to going through those pictures. Given how her investigation into her mother's death was going, they might be the only thing that came of her trip back to Carling Lake.

Daton may not have had time for breakfast, but Karine was starving. The café served breakfast and lunch, so she turned her attention to the menu above the counter and got in line.

"Karine? Karine Eloi?" Her head snapped to the left and her gaze landed on the woman behind the counter. It took a second for her to realize who it was.

"Meghan Foster?" Meghan had lived a few streets over and had been her regular babysitter when she was younger. She was only five or six years older than Karine, but she'd aged well. Her eyes were as clear and blue as the last time Karine had seen her, and her skin was clean, smooth and tanned, as if she'd just come back from days lazing on the beach. Her high blond ponytail swung as she wiped her hands on her apron and rounded the counter.

"I heard you were in town for a while." Meghan gave her a hug. "You look great."

"So do you. Wow, you look just like I remember you when I was twelve."

Meghan gave a hearty laugh. "I wish, but thank you."

"So, you work here," Karine said, taking in the apron with the OrganicSandwich name stitched across the front.

"I own it," Meghan said with a smile.

"Congrats."

"Thanks. My husband, Buck, and I started the shop several years ago. He'd been the manager at several stores around the county and he wanted something of his own. I wanted a job that allowed me some flexibility after our second child was born, so here we are."

"Well, it smells delicious. What would you suggest?"

"Today's breakfast special is a spinach, egg and cheese breakfast sandwich on a bagel."

"Sounds fabulous. I'll take it."

Meghan smiled and waved her to a table. "Have a seat and I'll bring it to you when it's ready. Would you like something to drink?"

Karine ordered a chai tea and grabbed the empty table by the front window. It was half past eight in the morning, but the shop was still doing a brisk business. Mostly takeout, but there was a handful of tables where patrons sat and ate too.

A younger woman who'd been behind the counter when she'd ordered brought her tea to the table. Karine scrolled on her phone until Meghan appeared with a plate in each hand.

"I hope you don't mind. I thought I could take a break and we could catch up."

"I don't mind at all. In fact, I hate to eat alone. You'd be saving me from some major embarrassment."

"Wonderful." Meghan set a plate down in front of Karine and scooted into the chair on the other side of the table.

They made small talk and ate for a while. Karine got the feeling that Meghan was working up to something and, when Meghan pushed her empty plate to the side and leaned forward, she knew she hadn't been wrong.

"The rumor around town is that you've been asking questions about your mother and the time period around when she was killed."

"That's the rumor?" Karine said noncommittally.

Meghan's smile was wry. "It is. I don't know if you knew, but I adored your mother. She was everything I wished my mother had been."

Karine had been pretty young, and not really observant as to what the adults or even older kids like Meghan might have been going through when she'd lived in Carling Lake. But it had been common knowledge that Meghan's mom, Cindy Streeter, was an alcoholic and less than attentive parent. Cindy had been fortunate enough to inherit a house from her parents, but Meghan and her younger brother had largely been left to raise themselves. Meghan had been the go-to babysitter for Karine's parents and her friends' parents, which she now realized had been their way of helping Meghan and her brother, of making sure that at least there was some money going to them that their mother wouldn't spend on booze.

Karine reached across the table and squeezed Meghan's hand. "I know she thought highly of you and she'd be so proud to see what you've accomplished."

"Yeah." Meghan's smile brightened. "I hope so." She cleared her throat. "There's something you don't know. Something I've never told anyone."

Karine's heart skipped a beat. "Okay."

Meghan picked up a paper napkin from the table and twisted it between her fingers. “I don’t know where to begin or how to tell this story. I’ve never told anyone. Not even Buck.”

Karine reached for her hand again. “Just start at the beginning.”

“The beginning. Okay. I guess, then, that would be my sophomore year in high school. I was a quiet kid. My mother’s drinking and erratic behavior had already taught me how to make myself small, invisible. I did well at school, but didn’t make any waves. I didn’t want to stand out, you know what I mean?”

“I think so, yes.”

“Except, I was a teenager, so I also did want to be noticed, you know. I don’t know how to explain it exactly.”

Karine chuckled. “You don’t have to explain being a teenage girl to me. I remember.”

Meghan laughed too. “I guess I don’t. It was a confusing time, I guess is the best way to describe it, so when Principal Howser started noticing me, it made me feel good. I actually didn’t think much of it at first, just like the principal saying hi in the hallway and stuff.”

Karine’s stomach turned, but she kept silent and just listened.

“And it was just that…for a while, hellos in the corridor between class or if he saw me after band practice. ‘Hi. How was band practice?’ ‘Did you have a good weekend?’ Like normal stuff. But I noticed that he always seemed to single me out. Like one time Vanessa Grey and her harpies—”

Karine made a face. The name didn’t ring any bells.

“Right, I forgot you were so much younger. Vanessa

Grey and her harpies were the Carling Lake equivalent of Regina George and the Plastics. The mean girls. Anyway, they were always kissing up to Mr. Howser and, frankly, he seemed to enjoy the attention. But all of a sudden, he was walking right past Vanessa and speaking to me in the halls."

Karine had a feeling she knew where this was going.

"Then he started calling me to his office. At first, I was terrified I was in trouble, but he said he was calling me in to 'check in.'" Meghan made air quotes. "But he never checked in on anyone else, as far as I knew. And he was doing it, like, a lot."

"Didn't any of the teachers notice?"

Meghan scoffed. "I'm sure they did. But no one ever said anything, not to me and not to Principal Howser, as far as I knew. He'd been hand-picked by the school board and you know how small-town power dynamics work. And I didn't have a parent who was going to go to bat for me."

She'd been vulnerable. The perfect target for a predator.

"Then he started touching me…nothing sexual," she hurried to add. "Just like massaging my shoulders. Patting my thigh. Brushing against my breast. I didn't know what to do."

"What happened?" Karine asked softly.

"Your mother." Meghan smiled wistfully. "I used to go into the woods behind your house just to think and be alone. To practice my clarinet because my mother hated the sound of it. I was in the woods one day, in a clearing that I thought only I knew about," she chuckled, "playing my clarinet. Mr. Howser had been escalating, and I was terrified of what he might do next. I didn't know what to do, or who to tell, or if anyone would believe me. It was eating away at me."

A single tear fell from her eye. "I don't know how long I was there before I eventually realized that I wasn't alone. Your mom was there with her easel, painting. I offered to leave, but she told me to stay because she'd enjoyed painting to the sound of music. I honestly don't know what possessed me to tell her what was going on, but it all just came out. We talked until the sun went down and then your mom walked me home."

Karine's heart pinched with love for her mother.

Meghan swiped at the tear. "Let me tell you, I was terrified of going to school on Monday morning. I knew your mom well enough to know that there was no way she was going to just ignore what I'd told her. But looking back now, I see that's exactly why I'd told her. Because I knew she'd help. I saw Principal Howser almost the minute I walked through the schoolhouse doors. I thought I was going to faint, but he took one look at me and turned the other way. Nearly ran down the hall in the opposite direction."

Karine's brow rose. "My mother did something."

Meghan raised her hands. "To this day, I don't know exactly what she did, but yes, she did something. That day, after I got home from school, your mom came by. She asked about my day and I told her that Principal Howser had steered clear of me. All she said was 'Good. You don't have to worry about him anymore.' She came by every day for the next couple of weeks. And then at the end of the month, the school sent home a notice that Principal Howser was taking a leave of absence to attend to some personal business. He never came back. In fact, I learned later that the school board had quietly voted to terminate his contract for cause and that Mr. Howser couldn't get a job with any of the surrounding school boards. That's why he took a job working construction."

And if Meghan was right about her mother having a hand in his firing, it explained the malevolence Martin had aimed at her at Barney's the other night. His dislike for her mother, no doubt, extended to her as well.

"He still practically runs when he sees me in town." Meghan's smile said she couldn't have been happier about that.

A scary thought bloomed in Karine's head. "Meghan, when did you say all this took place?"

"My sophomore year," Meghan answered somberly, giving her a moment to put all the pieces of the puzzle together. "Principal Howser was let go less than a month before your mother was murdered."

Chapter Seventeen

Karine hadn't answered the text Omar had sent her that morning, inviting her over for a pancake breakfast, and he'd taken that as a sign that she was worried about what had happened between them the night before. So he was surprised to find her on the other side of the door when he answered the doorbell.

"Karine." She was practically vibrating in front of him, whether it was with excitement or fear, he couldn't tell. "What's going on? Are you okay?"

"I'm fine. I ran into Meghan Foster at OrganicSandwich and she told me something about my mother."

He opened the door wider and Karine barreled past him and into the house. "Do you want some tea? Something to calm you down."

"I can't calm down," she said. "Meghan just told me that Martin Howser harassed her when she was a student at Carling Lake High and that she told my mother and that she thinks my mother got him fired."

"Whoa. Wait a minute. Slow down and start at the beginning."

She told him about meeting Daton at OrganicSandwich and running into Meghan, which didn't surprise him since he knew Meghan and her husband owned the organic sandwich shop. Her talk with Daton hadn't turned up anything helpful before he'd left. But Meghan had sat with her while she'd eaten breakfast and told her about Principal Howser's harassment, how Meghan had run into Marilee one day in the woods and revealed to her what was going on, and that Howser had immediately backed off, losing his job as principal not long after.

"Meghan said Principal Howser lost his job about a month before my mother was killed. Omar—" Karine grabbed him by the wrists "—this gives Martin Howser a motive to kill my mother."

"Slow down, Karine. We only have Meghan's side of the story."

Karine looked as if she was about to argue with him.

"And I'm not saying that she isn't telling the absolute truth, but even if everything she said is true, it's a big leap to accuse Martin Howser of murder just because he may blame your mother for costing him his job."

Karine glared at him. "What do you suggest I do, then?"

"Probably exactly what you've already planned to do. Talk to Howser. Confront him with what Meghan told you and see what he has to say. Gauge how he reacts."

Some of the anger in her eyes dimmed. "That was my next step, although, based on the dirty look Howser shot me outside of Barney's, I'm sure he isn't going to agree to meet with me, so I'm going to have to track him down first."

An ambush. Her plan was getting worse by the second.

"Okay. Well, I'm coming with you."

He'd expected her to say he didn't have to. That she could handle it alone. But instead, he got a relieved smile.

"Thanks. I'd appreciate that. Does that mean you don't have to work today? I know park rangers don't keep nine-to-five hours, but you've been helping me a lot these last few days. I meant it when I said I didn't want to get you in trouble."

"No, I'm off today and tomorrow. I'd actually planned to go on an overnight camping trek. I want to check something out in the northern part of the forest and it will just be easier to camp out and head back tomorrow."

She frowned. "It might rain this evening."

He shrugged. "It wouldn't be the first time I've camped in the rain. I have a waterproof tent. I'll be fine."

"Why the sudden desire to go camping?"

They hadn't talked much about his work since she'd arrived in town, but now he filled her in quickly on the possible water contamination.

"I've been a terrible friend," she said. "You have this major thing happening at your job and I didn't even know about it."

"You've been a great friend," he said, tripping over the last word. She was so much more than a friend.

"You have a lot going on right now and I get it. I just need to do this one thing and, like I said, it shouldn't take more than an overnight. I've been giving it a lot of thought and, if I'm right, about a pollutant—"

"You know the Carling Lake Forest better than anyone. If you say something unnatural is causing these animals to get sick and die, then something is."

He savored the sensation her belief in him brought on. "It has to be coming from the northern sector. It's isolated enough that if someone is dumping chemicals or something up there, no one would know. I'm not sure how they'd be doing it though." His body tensed with frustration. "It's nearly impossible to get through those dense woods on anything but foot."

Karine pointed at him. "Nearly impossible isn't impossible."

"True."

"How long has it been since you've been up there?"

"It's been a while."

"So someone might have cut a path."

He ceded the point. "It's possible. The main road is several miles away, but on an ATV, someone could cut a trail through."

"So we hike up there and take a look."

Omar's eyebrows rose. "We?"

"Yes. We. You've got my back. I've got your back. You've been helping me out with my investigation into my mother's death. This is the least I can do to repay you."

"You don't need to repay me. I want to help you."

She pinned him with her gaze. "And I want to help you."

A charged moment passed between them.

It was shattered by someone banging on the front door.

Omar opened a drawer in the side table next to the door and took out his service weapon. He shot a hard glance at Karine. "Go into the kitchen."

He waited until she did before he went to the door.

The person on the other side banged again.

He glanced out of the living room window at the same time that the person spoke.

"Monroe! Open up. It's the sheriff's department," Shep called out.

He exhaled a sigh of relief. He slid the gun back into the drawer and opened the door.

"Deputy Coben. What can I do for you?"

Deputy Coben scowled. "I've had a complaint about you and Miss Eloi. Tried knocking on her door, but no one answered. Do you have any idea where she is?"

"I'm here, Deputy." Karine stepped out of the kitchen and came to stand next to Omar.

Coben's smile turned into a smirk.

Omar fought the urge to wipe it off his face. "What can we help you with, Deputy Coben?" he gritted out.

"Richie Portman says you two have been harassing him."

"We spoke to him about what he might have seen on the night my mother was murdered and offered our support at the hospital. We did not harass anyone," Karine said.

Shep glowered. "I told you, looking into your mother's murder was a bad idea."

"And I disagree," Karine snapped back. "I'm not breaking any laws, so I don't see what business it is of yours, Deputy."

That statement wasn't entirely true, but Omar wasn't going to correct her.

"If Richie Portman had seen something relevant to your mother's murder, the sheriff's department would have found out and pursued it," Coben snarled.

"Except you didn't." Karine seemed on the verge of screaming.

Omar reached out and laid what he hoped was a calming hand on her shoulder. He didn't want her to say too much to Shep. The deputy couldn't stop them from investigating, but the less he knew, the better, as far as he was concerned.

Coben's eyes darkened. "What does that mean?"

"Nothing," Omar said.

"We found a recording that shows someone sneaking around my parents' house on the night of my mother's murder, and Richie, or someone in Richie's house, in a window, who might have been watching at the time."

Omar groaned internally.

"A recording? Where did you find this video?"

Karine seemed to realize a moment too late that she'd said too much. She shot a cornered glance at Omar.

He turned away from Karine and looked at the deputy. "I found it. In Amber Spindler's house."

"Amber Spindler's... What the hell were you doing in her house?"

"I wanted to take a look around. See if I could figure out what she wanted to tell Karine."

"You interfered with a crime scene," Shep growled.

"No, I didn't. The sheriff's department is treating Amber's death as a suspected suicide or accidental death. I presumed the sheriff's department had completed its search, as the house wasn't cordoned off."

"Oh, yeah," Shep said somewhat pathetically. "Well, I know for a fact the house was locked up. How did you get in?"

Omar hesitated, purposely keeping his gaze from straying to Karine, although he could feel her eyes on him. He didn't want to lie, but he wouldn't implicate her in a crime.

So, he remained silent.

"Where is this recording now? It's evidence in an open case, and you are obstructing justice by not turning it over to the sheriff's department."

Karine scowled, but reached into her purse and pulled out the disc copy, slapping it into Shep's hand. "Some people might ask why, in twenty-three years, the sheriff's department never discovered this recording?"

Shep's face turned purple and he pointed a stubby finger at Karine. "I'm going to tell you two this one more time. Stop sticking your nose where it doesn't belong or you might just get it cut clean off."

"It was my mother who was killed," Karine said. "I'd say my nose is right where it belongs."

"Deputy Coben, did Richie file a formal harassment complaint?"

Shep stared at Karine, but when she didn't back down, he finally shifted his glare to Omar. "No, which you should be grateful for. But I'm telling you to convince your girlfriend there to stop her snooping around before she crosses the wrong person."

"Well, you've delivered your missive like a good little messenger deputy. I think it's time for you to leave. You have a good day." Omar slid the door forward.

Shep slammed his hand against it, stopping it from closing. He was practically vibrating with anger. "You better get smart real fast, Monroe. If you don't, you and your lady friend might just find yourselves in a heap of trouble."

Chapter Eighteen

Omar didn't have any idea where Martin Howser lived, but he knew that the former principal now worked as the foreman at a local construction company. Karine hadn't been sure about approaching the man at his job, but Omar pointed out it would be safer to approach him in a public, or at least semipublic, place.

Omar drove them to the construction company's office, located in the industrial park off the main highway.

"You know I'm starting to wonder if there's more to Shep's determination to stop us from looking into your mother's murder than just keeping a lid on his shoddy police work," Omar said, making a right into the industrial park. According to his GPS, the company was located at the rear of the industrial complex.

"Something like what?"

"That's the question." He turned the pickup into the parking lot of Ace's Construction Company.

Howser walked out of the building in front of them and headed for one of the truck bays at the side of the building.

"There's Martin Howser."

Together, they got out of Omar's truck and walked toward Howser.

"Mr. Howser." She stepped in front of Howser, stopping him as he headed for the rear of the closest rig. "Karine Eloi."

He scowled, his gaze bouncing over Omar then back to Karine. "I know who you are."

"I'm wondering if I can have a moment of your time."

"What for?"

"I'd like to ask you a few questions. About when you were principal at Carling Lake High."

"That part of my life is over." He tried to step away, but Omar put a hand to his chest, stopping him.

Howser's scowl deepened. Howser may have been twenty years older than she and Omar, but his work in construction had kept him fit and muscled. The last thing she wanted was for this conversation to turn physical.

Since Howser wasn't inclined to give her time to ease into the thornier questions, Karine decided to dive into the deep end.

"Meghan Foster told me about what you did to her when she was in high school. And how my mother intervened."

"I don't know what Meghan Foster told you—" Howser took a threatening step forward.

Omar again pressed a hand to Howser's chest. "That's close enough."

"Meghan told me you harassed her. She told my mother, and you were let go from the school system soon after."

"That little—"

Omar made a noise deep in his throat, cutting Howser off.

Howser glared at them. "Whatever Meghan Foster told you is a lie. But your mother believed her and this town—"

Howser shot a disdainful look around, but there was no one near except them. "This town adored your mother and grandfather. People around here thought they walked on water."

Someone hadn't adored her mom. Someone had killed her and, based on the venom coming from Martin Howser, he could very well be that someone.

"She convinced the board to fire me based on the word of a child," Howser continued. "Everyone knows how confused teenage girls can get. Especially girls like Meghan. No father in the home. Her mother is a drunk. Nobody pays her any attention, so of course when I show her the least little bit of attention, she misinterprets it."

"Misinterprets," Omar growled.

Howser continued to glare, but he also took a step back.

Karine crowded into Howser's personal space, taking advantage of his discomfort. "Maybe you decided to get back at my mother for ruining your career. You waited until you thought she was home alone and then you confronted her. Maybe you didn't even mean to kill her and things just got out of hand. You lost your temper."

"Now just wait a damn minute." Howser's face went red as a tomato. "I didn't kill anyone. I despised your mother for ruining my life. My wife left me. Took my son. I lost my job. My house. My family. But I'm not a murderer, and you better not be starting any rumors otherwise."

She looked Howser in the eye. "I'm not looking for rumors. I want facts. I'm going to find out who killed my mother."

"Well, I can't help you any more than telling you it wasn't me. Now, I've got better things to do."

Howser went to step around her, but Karine moved with him, blocking his way.

"You're a scumbag, Howser, and I promise you this. If you killed my mother, I will see you behind bars for it. You can count on it."

Chapter Nineteen

"Are you sure you're up for this?" Omar asked as they neared the turnoff that would take them to the trailhead.

"For the tenth time, I'm sure," Karine responded. "It will be good for me. I need time to think and process everything I've heard about my mother and her murder since I've arrived in town. This will be a good time to think."

"It's been several eventful days," he said, thinking about the kiss they'd shared.

The area of the Carling Lake Forest that they were planning to hike wasn't a popular spot for camping in no small part because of how difficult it was to reach. Omar drove them to the northernmost parking lot, which was empty. They got out and went to the back of the pickup. He'd put the cover on the truck bed, but they didn't need much. His job as a ranger meant he was as familiar with the forest as he was with his own home, but he and Karine had spent their childhood camping, hiking and exploring these woods.

They slung their packs onto their backs and started out.

He stole glances at Karine as she kept pace beside him. She wore a tight tank top that accentuated her ample breasts underneath a lightweight long-sleeved shirt. Well-worn blue jeans sculpted her tight behind. He found the mountain woman look sexy as hell. He found her sexy as hell.

"Penny for your thoughts." Karine was watching him.

"Oh, nothing," he said, feeling heat crawl up his neck. He hoped she hadn't noticed. "I'm just thinking about the best place to set up camp for the night. What about you? You've been pretty quiet."

They'd been hiking for more than an hour and they'd barely spoken a word.

"I'm just thinking about Martin Howser." She hesitated for a moment. "And my father."

"I wondered when you'd be ready to talk about that."

"I just can't believe he cheated on my mother."

"Don't shoot the messenger, but I hear that marriage can be hard," he said teasingly.

Karine rolled her eyes. "I know marriage is hard."

Omar raised an eyebrow.

"Not from experience, but you know what I mean. I just… I know my dad isn't perfect, but I wouldn't have ever predicted he'd betray my mother. They had their problems. I mean, they were an odd couple from the first, but my dad is like the most honest person I've ever met."

They stepped over a fallen log.

"You know your dad. Maybe he just made a mistake. He and your mom might have worked things out. Did you talk to him about it?"

She shook her head. "No, it… I was just so shocked and I wasn't sure what I was feeling. I just didn't want to be around him, so I left."

"I can understand that, but you know you're going to have to talk to your dad sometime."

"Sometime," she repeated.

But from the sound of it, sometime wouldn't be anytime soon.

They walked on for another hour, but the topics stayed out of the emotional or controversial areas of their lives.

They finally reached the stream that he wanted to take a sample from. It was one of the many ephemeral streams in the forest, but when its flow was heavy, the water had the capacity to travel quite a distance. It was also not far from the spot he'd picked out for them to camp for the night.

"So you think this stream could be feeding into other streams and creeks downhill and poisoning the smaller animals, right?" Karine asked, slinging her pack off her back and dropping it to the ground at the side of the stream.

He'd explained the details of his theory about the poisoned water on their hike to the stream.

"Pretty much." He was crouched down at the stream's edge, preparing to take a sample of the water. Fortunately, it was still full from the rain shower two nights before.

"But I thought you said the tests you'd had done on the downhill streams came back clean."

"They did," he said tightly.

"Sooooo."

"I just want to be sure. It's possible that because those larger water bodies receive incoming water from multiple smaller sources, there just wasn't enough contaminant to be detected in the water. Yet."

Omar put a cap on the second tube of water and tucked it into his pack along with the first sample he'd taken. Since John wasn't going to order another test, he planned to pay for the tests out of his own pocket. He'd have to call in a favor, but his friend who worked at a private environmental testing lab thought he could get the tests done. Omar just needed to make sure he had enough of the sample.

"'Yet,'" Karine parroted. "Have you considered sources of pollution other than water?"

He looked up at her from his crouched position. "What do you mean?"

"Well, I am admittedly not an expert, but I am the daughter of a botanist. Have you considered the soil?"

"The soil?"

"Yeah. The animals you mentioned you found, several of them are burrowers. And even the birds. They sometimes make nests in the hollow bases of trees or eat little creatures that are burrowers. If it's the soil that's contaminated, they'd be affected."

She was right. He'd gotten it into his head that it was the water that was contaminated because he'd found the animals near water bodies, but that could be a coincidence or an effect of the pollutant.

He'd brought more vials than he could have ever needed. He took two out of his pack and filled them both with soil.

"I'm not sure if my friend's lab can test soil samples, but even if his doesn't, I'll find one that will."

He packed the vials away with the water samples and stood, hiking his pack onto his back.

Karine reached down for her pack. Her right leg slid out from under her. Her arms windmilled.

He reached out, grabbed her by the forearms and steadied her, pulling her to him.

A sizzling awareness pulsated between them.

Karine's eyes were trained on his lips and he was pretty sure he was reading her mind.

She wanted to kiss him. Maybe as much as he wanted to kiss her right now.

Without thinking, he took a step forward at the same time she stepped back out of his arms.

"Thanks," she said, looking away.

He moved back.

She hoisted her backpack. "We should get going, don't you think? It will be getting dark soon, and we still need to set up camp." She turned away.

He took a deep breath and let it out slowly. There was no cold shower in the forest, so he fought to get his libido in check. "The spot I have in mind is not far from here."

He led the way and they made it to the clearing he had in mind without incident.

Karine might have lived in the big city now, but she hadn't forgotten how to set up camp.

She took charge of setting up their tents while he made their dinner, soup and several pieces of artisan bread, using a backpacking stove.

"Ah, we have a small problem," Karine said.

He turned.

Karine held the two flaps of her tent. "The zipper on the front flaps is broken."

"I guess we should have checked them before we left. That's what I get for being in a rush."

"I could still use it, but if it rains tonight, it could get pretty wet inside."

"Even if it doesn't rain, it will be cold if you can't zip up. You can have my tent. I'll sleep under the stars."

"You'll sleep under the cold, rainy stars." She shook her head. "That doesn't make sense." She hesitated. "If you're okay with it, we can share your tent. It's big enough."

His tent was large enough for two, but it would be snug. His groin twitched at the thought of Karine sleeping a breath away from him.

"I'm okay with it."

They ate, sticking to neutral topics of discussion. But that didn't stop the sexual awareness from crackling between them.

After dinner, they washed up, securing their gear and settling into their sleeping bags only minutes before the light pattering of rain drummed on the tent's roof.

He lay still and stiff as a board in his sleeping bag next to Karine, the smell of her perfume, which had always reminded him of the ocean, mingling with the scent of the forest.

Sleep was elusive. He couldn't turn his mind off. Or away from thoughts of taking Karine into his arms. Kissing her. Stripping her of her clothes and exploring her body thoroughly. He was sure she felt the electricity between them whenever they were alone. And he was equally certain that the same thing that kept him from acting on it had kept her from acting on it. Their friendship. He never wanted to lose her as a friend, but he couldn't keep pretending that he didn't want her as more either.

As he lay there listening to the rain, he realized Karine was struggling to fall asleep as well.

She shifted onto her side, looking at him.

"What?" he asked.

"What would you do if I kissed you right now?"

That had not been what he'd expected her to say.

She didn't wait for him to respond. She lunged across the tent, grabbing him by his shirt and pressing her lips to his. He gave in to the kiss, desire coursing through him.

She rolled so that she was on top of him. He ran his fingers through her hair, drawing her in as close as they could get with clothes between them. He knew she could feel how much he wanted her. He wanted to be inside her, but he had to make sure she was sure.

He pulled back enough to look into her eyes. "Karine?"

She gazed at him, desire darkening her eyes. She flicked her tongue over her bottom lip and said, "Yes. I want this."

That was all he needed to hear.

He took her lips again and stopped thinking about the wisdom of what they were about to do and started to just feel.

KARINE WAS BREATHING HARD. Excitement and desire coursed through her. Throwing herself, literally, at Omar was impulsive, but she'd wanted him for a long time. Longer than she was probably ready to admit to herself.

And now, here they were, limbs entangled, lips pressed together, the heat between them ready to combust.

Omar slipped his hand under her shirt and kneaded her breast beneath her bra. Her nipples tightened into tight beads under his touch. She moaned.

"You are so sexy," he said against her lips.

Her blood raced. She felt as if she were speeding down a steep hill without brakes. She was going to crash, but she didn't care. The ride was worth it.

Omar grabbed the hem of his shirt and whipped it over his head while she shrugged out of her top.

Omar eased her from the rest of her clothes then made short work of his own.

"You're perfect." His eyes roamed over every inch of her skin, sending electric shocks throughout her body.

He ran a finger over a birthmark on her hip.

She trembled. "If you keep this up, I might combust."

"That's the idea."

His fingers were like magic. Tickling, teasing and finally finding her core.

She arched against him.

It didn't take long before she felt the waves of ecstasy pull her under.

Omar sheathed himself as she breathlessly rode the last surges of bliss.

She didn't have time to catch her breath before he was back, braced atop her.

He seated himself inside her easily, as if he belonged there. As if he were home.

She shuddered at the weightiness of the thought. And then she wasn't thinking at all. She could only feel.

Pleasure rippled through her. She shifted to take him in deeper and they both moaned in synchronized ecstasy.

"Open your eyes, Karine. Look at me."

She did, the connection between them heightening even more.

She'd had intense sex before, but never like this. This, she knew, she'd only ever have with one man.

Omar.

Omar, who knew her better than anyone.

Omar, who knew all about her past.

Omar, who got her like no one else ever had.

Omar, who was right where he should be. With her.

He quickened his pace and she knew they were both close. He surged once, twice, and then her body tightened and she let out a sharp cry as he drove them both over the edge.

Omar collapsed next to her, pulling her to him as he did.

Her heart pounded hard against his. She ran her fingers through the hair on his chest.

She couldn't ever remember feeling shy after intercourse, but that was exactly how she felt now. Shy. Unsure.

Omar ran his hand over the birthmark on her hip. "I never knew you had a birthmark."

"You've never seen me this naked."

His body shook with laughter and her awkwardness eased.

"I've never seen you naked at all before, but you are one of the most beautiful things I have ever seen."

She stared at his very fine abdominal muscles. "I'm sure you say that to every woman you—"

He tipped her chin up with his index finger. "I have never lied to you and I will never lie to you. You are the most beautiful woman I've ever known."

She leaned up and kissed him.

He cupped her backside and she entwined her legs with his, feeling the fire ignite within her again.

Omar rolled her onto her back, but a fleeting thought floated through her mind before she lost herself in his touch for a second time.

What about tomorrow?

Chapter Twenty

Omar woke alone. He shrugged into his clothes and boots and pushed the tent flaps back, stepping outside. The sun had already broken over the horizon, its rays shining down on the forest floor through the trees. The rain from the night before had cooled the air, sharpening the smell of soil and pine, and softening the ground beneath his feet.

He scanned the clearing where they'd set up camp. "Karine?"

For a brief moment, he wondered if she'd gotten up early and left camp alone. But her pack and all their gear was still there.

"I'm here." Her voice came from just inside the tree line. "Out in a second."

He grabbed a sweatshirt from his pack, pulling it over his head as Karine stepped from the trees.

"Good morning."

"Good morning," she replied without looking at him.

His heart sank. Last night had been everything he'd dreamed of and more, but if she was having regrets… "Are we okay?"

"Yes, of course we are," she said without meeting his gaze.

Of course.

They ate breakfast and started the reverse hike out of the woods in almost complete silence, and not the comfortable, friendly silence from their hike the day before. This was an awkward, cringe-inducing quietness that left questions swirling in his mind. He'd thought their night together had been incredible. After Karine had fallen asleep in his arms, he'd lain awake fantasizing about how they could make a relationship work. It hadn't entered his mind that she might not have felt the same way about crossing the line from friends to lovers as he did.

And if she didn't feel the same? Could he continue to be her friend, her best friend, when every part of him wanted to be more?

The questions bandied through his head as they walked. They were almost back to the truck when he couldn't take the questions any longer. One way or the other, he had to know what she was thinking. What she felt.

He pulled up short. "What happened between us last night?"

A part of him knew that things would never be the same between them. No matter what she answered, their relationship had changed and there was no going back. But he hoped…

Karine's gaze skittered away from him. "Last night was…a mistake."

Mistake. The word cut through him like a knife.

"Listen, what happened last night… We've been friends for a long time, like, almost thirty years. That's amazing and incredible. And I don't want to lose our friendship."

"Friendship."

His brain felt as if it had been filled with cotton. A mistake. Friendship. He imagined being shot would have been less painful than hearing those words from her after what he'd felt making love to her.

She let out a heavy sigh. "Yes, friendship. We're both adults and last night was…it was great. But it doesn't have to be a big deal. I'm going to go back to Los Angeles and you live here." She finally looked him in the eye, reaching out and pressing her palm against his heart. "This can be one amazing night we shared and that we remember fondly, as friends."

He recognized the unfamiliar pang in his chest as heartbreak. He'd done his best to avoid the feeling by keeping his romantic relationships with women at the surface level. It had been easy because he'd given his heart away years ago. To Karine. And he'd never gotten it back.

And now she was saying she didn't want it.

His entire body felt as if it had grown twenty pounds heavier than it had been just moments ago. Each of Karine's words had added a weight that he wasn't sure any amount of time in the gym would get rid of.

But if this was what she wanted, there was nothing he wouldn't do to make her happy. Even walk away from her.

Because that was what he'd have to do when she left for Los Angeles this time. Walk away. A clean break. He couldn't go on pretending that he just wanted to be her best friend when he wanted so much more.

How to do that without shattering into a thousand pieces himself was something he'd have to work out later. "Of course. You're right. Our friendship means too much to jeopardize it."

Karine's face flashed with something he might have

pegged as disappointment under other circumstances. She gave him a tepid smile.

Neither of them spoke again until he pulled to a stop in front of her house. He left the engine idling as he got out and retrieved her gear from the back of the truck.

She looked at him with a question in her eyes. “Omar—”

“I need to go,” he said, cutting off whatever she was going to say. He wasn’t sure he could stand to hear whatever soothing words she was going to trot out. He got it. She wasn’t interested in being more than friends. Maybe he was being a little petulant about it, but it hurt.

“Oh, well… I’ll see you tomorrow, then?”

He began backing toward the driver’s-side door. “I don’t know. I have to work tomorrow and I need to get these samples to my friend in Stunnersville.” He turned to get into the pickup.

“Omar, please, wait,” Karine said.

He faced her again.

“I don’t want things to be weird between us. Can’t we just pretend last night never happened and go back to the way things were?”

“What if I don’t want to go back?” He slammed his palm against the side of the truck. “What if last night meant something to me, even if it didn’t to you?”

“I—”

“I can’t make you have feelings for me, but I can’t pretend anymore that I don’t have feelings for you. Because I do. I don’t want to just be your best friend. I want to be your lover, your partner, your—”

He stopped himself. He’d never seen Karine look more terrified.

"I'm sorry. I… I just can't," she whispered.

He jumped into the truck, not waiting for her to respond. He didn't know how he was going to get through the rest of Karine's stay in Carling Lake, but right now he knew he needed space.

Space from the woman he wanted nothing more than to hold close.

Chapter Twenty-One

Karine grabbed the strawberry ice cream from her freezer and padded in her slippers and pajamas into the living room. She'd spent the day spinning her wheels regarding the investigation into her mother's death. She'd made no progress on identifying the person Amber had had dinner with the night she'd died. Martin Howser had a motive to kill her mother, but she knew that wouldn't be enough to jump-start the sheriff's department's investigation. And, if Becky or Richie Portman had seen anything the night of her mother's murder, they still weren't willing to share it with her or the sheriff. On top of all that, she'd been brooding about her argument with Omar.

She'd picked up the phone dozens of times to call him, but she'd never gone through with the call. What was there to say? He wanted to be more than her friend, and she didn't see him that way.

Well, that wasn't true. She'd definitely seen him as more than a friend the night they'd gone camping. She'd had lovers before, of course, but none of them had ever made her feel as much as she had in Omar's arms.

It couldn't work between them. She lived in Los Angeles and he lived here in Carling Lake. She wasn't a country girl and he wasn't a city guy. More than that, she risked losing him as a friend for a fleeting romance.

What if it isn't fleeting?

She'd never been good at romantic relationships. Too independent. Too career-oriented. She'd never had a relationship that had lasted beyond a year. She couldn't risk that with Omar.

They could get over this bump and back to their friendship. She closed her eyes and breathed through the ache in her chest.

They had to.

SHE SETTLED DOWN on the sofa and found *Krull* on Netflix, but not even a young Liam Neeson in one of her favorite sci-fi movies could pull her out of her funk. She glanced out the window as the final credits started to roll.

She rose and went to close the curtains.

A silver sedan rolled to a stop in front of the house. She was surprised to see her father unfold from the driver's side of the car.

He caught her watching from inside the house and waved.

She closed the blinds and went to open the front door.

"Dad, what are you doing here?"

He stopped on the top porch step. "I couldn't stop thinking about how we left things the other day. I didn't like it. Can we talk?"

She stood aside so he could step into the house.

He froze just inside the door, looking down the hall. She didn't have to imagine what he was seeing.

"Why don't we go into the living room?" She placed a

hand lightly on his shoulder and guided him away from the memories of the past.

Her father let out a shuddering breath as they crossed into the living room. "This is the first time I've been in this house since… Everything looks so different. The furniture is all new."

She wasn't in any mood for small talk. She wasn't in the mood for a conversation at all with her father, but he'd driven for hours to talk to her and today seemed to be her day to have intense, emotional conversations with her loved ones.

"Dad."

"Right. I didn't come to assess the decor. Come. Sit with me." He sat and patted the spot next to him on the sofa.

She sat, and he took her hand in his.

Her father swallowed, his Adam's apple bobbing. "This is harder than I imagined it would be."

"Why did you cheat on Mom?"

"You know your mother was only twenty-one when we met. Fresh out of college. I was almost ten years older and, frankly, I hadn't had very much experience with the ladies." He chuckled. "We were infatuated with each other. And then we had you and we both fell in love with you."

"So you stayed together for me?"

"Yes and no. We stayed together because we both wanted what was best for you, certainly, but I think we stayed together because it was easier than being apart in a lot of ways. Easier than proving all the people who thought we wouldn't last right. And because we were scared of what our lives would look like on the other side of making a decision to separate."

Despite the anger she felt toward her father, his words resonated. Wasn't that exactly why she was hesitant to move her relationship with Omar out of the friend zone? Standing still seemed so much safer.

"That doesn't explain why you had an affair."

"I met Stephanie during a difficult period in my life, but meeting her was a blessing and we fell in love. I won't apologize for that." He looked her in the eye. "If you ever fall in love, and I hope you do, you'll see how hard it is to walk away from that person. How hard you'd fight to be with them."

Karine's eyes cut toward Omar's house even though there was no way she could see it from where she stood. Would she? Would she fight for the person she loved? All signs pointed to no. Maybe some people were always just too scared to take the risk.

Not that she was in love with Omar. She couldn't be, despite what they'd shared. They were friends. Best friends.

She forced herself to focus on what her father was telling her. That he'd had a reason to get rid of her mother.

"You were going to dump Mom. But I guess her murder saved you from having to have that uncomfortable conversation, didn't it?" She turned her back on him. It was difficult to look at him with the thoughts she had running through her mind. Questions she needed to know the answers to, but was terrified to ask.

Her father pushed to his feet. "Karine," he said, his voice hard, "I know this is a lot for you to take in, but I am still your father."

She spun around to face him. "Did you kill Mom?"

Her father looked stunned. "Karine, I can't believe you would ask me such a thing." Hurt flashed across his face.

She crossed her arms over her chest in an effort to stop the trembling in her body. She could let it go. His shock had seemed genuine. So had the hurt she'd seen flash across his face. But he hadn't answered the question. Not really. And now that it was out there, the desire to hear him say yes or no was too strong to ignore.

"Did you kill my mother? Answer the question."

"No," her father snapped, his eyes hard pebbles.

She searched his face for a sign that he was telling her the truth. He looked angry enough to spit nails, but was that because he was appalled that she could even suggest that he'd killed his wife or because he was afraid she'd see through his lies?

She couldn't tell. Over the years, the distance that had grown between her and her father had made it nearly impossible for her to read him. And now she wasn't even sure she knew him at all.

After a long moment, her father let out a slow, deep breath. He seemed to shrink in on himself as the air left his lungs. "I know that you have had a lot thrown at you recently. I'm so sorry you found out about your mother's and my problems this way. You were so young when your mother died and after Stephanie and I married, I knew you never really warmed up to her. I didn't see any reason to drive a wedge further between you and her or me and you."

Was that all her father's omission was? An attempt to protect himself from embarrassment? She wanted to believe that, but there was no denying that the affair gave him, and Stephanie, a motive for wanting her mother out of the way.

“I need to get home,” her father said. “This trip was a spur-of-the-moment thing and Stephanie will be worried about me.”

He walked to the door and she followed.

Her father opened the front door, but turned back to her before stepping outside.

“I love you. You are, and always have been, the most important person in my life, and I’m sorry I haven’t always acted like it, but I would never intentionally hurt you.” He reached for her hand and this time she let him take it. He squeezed. “I’ll call you in a couple of days, okay?”

His last words were said almost as a plea.

She didn’t know how much she believed of what her father had told her, but she knew she wasn’t ready to cut him out of her life, so she nodded. She watched him amble down the walkway and get into his car, wondering how it was that getting an answer to her questions had somehow only left her with more questions.

OMAR DROVE DOWN the highway, back toward Carling Lake. He’d turned the samples over to his friend, Brett, who used to work for the state crime lab, but had recently gotten a job at a large private lab that could run every kind of environmental and agricultural test known to man. Brett had assured him he could have the test results within twenty-four hours.

They’d also spent a few hours chatting over beers. Brett’s wife had recently given birth to their first child, and Omar had had to coo over a lot of cute baby photos. Thankfully, Brett was so enamored with his new daughter that he hadn’t noticed that Omar wasn’t revealing very much about his own life. Omar was pretty sure Brett at least suspected his feelings for Karine were more than friendly, but he didn't want to rain on his friend's parade with the story of his disastrous love life.

He wound down the window and let the air flow over him, cooling the despair that heated his cheeks.

He'd bared his soul to Karine. Finally told her how he'd really felt about her, and she'd said "thanks, but no thanks." It hurt. It hurt so much it felt like the pain might kill him, but he'd have to get over it. The thing was, he didn't think he could get over Karine and be her best friend. That meant he'd have to let her go.

He would have thought his heart couldn't hurt any more, but it cracked into a million extra tiny little pieces. Karine would always be special to him, but he needed to learn how to imagine a future with someone other than her. Maybe then they could find a way back to being friends.

He pressed down on the accelerator and the pickup surged forward.

Maybe.

Chapter Twenty-Two

It was the smoke that woke her. She'd never been a smoker, so that was one way the smell was out of place. The other was that it didn't smell like cigarette smoke.

Karine opened her eyes and found a haze hovering over her bed. She swung her feet onto the floor and found it warm, although not unbearably so.

Something was wrong, but her brain was still too wrapped up in the fog of sleep for her to make out exactly what.

She slid her feet into slippers and shrugged into her robe before heading downstairs.

The smoke was thicker down there. One glance in the kitchen explained why.

Orange flames climbed up the walls and engulfed the cabinets.

The sound of the fire crackling and the wood it engulfed splintering filled the air, but the fire alarm was silent. She hadn't checked to make sure it was working when she'd arrived, and now it looked like she was paying the price.

She turned toward the front door, but pulled up short when she realized the flames seemed to have blanketed the front of the house too. She was boxed in by the fire. But that didn't make sense. How could the flames have jumped from the back of the house to the front without reaching the area where she now stood?

Logical or not, she had to get out. Now.

Smoke filled her lungs, sending a rough, hacking cough through her. Caution from a long-ago safety lecture ran through her mind.

It's the smoke that gets you, not the fire.

Out. She needed to get out now. If she couldn't go through the front or the back, what were her options?

She could go back upstairs, try jumping from a window. But the second-floor windows were quite a ways off the ground. She'd almost certainly injure herself. But a window wasn't a bad idea. Getting to the large front window in the living room meant going through the foyer, which, given the size of the flames, didn't seem wise.

But there was a smaller window in the formal dining room that might work.

A hacking cough gripped her. The smoke around her head was getting darker by the second.

Crawl.

Smoke rose and, in a fire, the best thing to do was to stay below it.

She went to her knees, the smoke still sending a wracking cough through her body.

Another memory from a long-ago fire safety lecture arose.

It doesn't take long for smoke inhalation to incapacitate a person.

She crawled into the dining room.

The smoke wasn't as thick in there, thank God, but she still stayed on her hands and knees.

Which wall was the window on?

Fear and panic joined the smoke in clogging her thoughts. She needed to calm down. Panicking wasn't going to help. In fact, it might get her killed.

Karine pictured the room in her mind's eyes. She was at the door. The window was on the wall directly across from the entry. She just needed to crawl straight ahead and the window should be right there.

She moved forward, stopping once to take control of a hacking cough.

The smoke was getting thicker, she realized when she bumped into a chair she hadn't seen until too late.

The fire was coming for her. She was running out of time.

After what seemed like much too long, she finally reached the other side of the room. She ran her hand up the wall until she reached the windowsill and pulled herself up.

She flicked the lock and tried to push the window up, but it wouldn't budge. Years of paint, rust and who knew what else had sealed it shut.

A coughing fit threatened to take over. She shrugged out of her robe, ripped one of the sleeves off, and pressed it to her nose and mouth. The makeshift mask made it marginally easier to breathe, but she knew that wouldn't last for long.

She needed something to break the window with. She turned, but the room was cloudy with smoke now. She couldn't see more than a step or two in front of her.

"Karine!"

She turned back to the window. Omar was on the other side, his face a desperate mask of terror.

"It's stuck," she called back. "I can't get it open."

"Stand to the side of the window."

She did as he ordered. A moment later, a paving brick shattered the glass.

Through the now shattered window, she could hear the shriek of the fire engines.

Omar knocked the remaining shards of glass from the window with an arm he'd wrapped in his T-shirt. She snatched up her torn robe from the floor and helped him clear the last piece of the broken glass.

He grabbed her arms and helped her through the window.

Somewhere in the quest to escape the fire, she'd lost her slippers. Her feet barely touched the grass before Omar swung her up into his arms.

A fire engine screeched to a stop in front of the house, followed by an ambulance.

Omar carried her to the ambulance and lifted her inside after one of the EMTs opened the rig's rear doors. He sat her on a gurney and took the seat across from her.

"Was there anyone else inside?" one of the firefighters asked from outside the ambulance.

She shook her head. "No." The single word was enough to bring on a coughing fit.

"Don't try to speak," Omar said.

"He's right," the EMT, a beefy man with a mop of curly blond hair, seconded. "Let's get the oxygen mask on you. Breath deep." He fit the mask over her face.

Deputy Coben jogged up to the rig as the EMT fitted a clamp over her thumb. The machine next to the gurney began to emit quick, rhythmic beeps while two separate lines danced across the screen. Her heart rate and oxygen levels.

"Everyone okay?" Deputy Coben asked in a huff.

Omar stood and stalked, slightly hunched over, toward the deputy, but didn't get out of the ambulance. "No, everyone is not okay. Someone set fire to Karine's house and nearly killed her!"

Deputy Coben threw up his hands. "Whoa, there now. We don't know for sure that this was arson."

The deputy's word hit her like a punch to the chest. *Arson.*

"We don't? When I saw the flames, I tried getting into the house by the front and the back doors," Omar said. "There were flames at both ends of the house. How do you explain that?"

All four of them turned to look at the house. It was all but engulfed now. Impossible to say where the fire had started without an expert opinion, but she had seen the flames firsthand. Omar was right. The fire had been in the front and back of the house, but not at the center. That didn't seem possible unless…unless someone had purposely started two separate fires with the intention of trapping her inside.

Karine's stomach knotted into a ball. Someone had tried to kill her. More than likely the same someone who'd killed her mother.

"Let's let the fire department do its job," Deputy Coben said.

The look Omar shot the deputy was enough to send the man backing up a step. Or two.

"If you'd done your job years ago, maybe there wouldn't still be a killer out there. Maybe this wouldn't have happened."

Deputy Coben's face pinked and his eyes narrowed to slits. "Now you just wait a damn minute, Monroe."

"Stop!" Karine said as forcefully as she could through the mask. "This is not helping anyone."

Omar shot one more venomous glance at Deputy Coben before reclaiming his seat across from Karine. She reached for his hand and gave it a squeeze. She could see that his anger at the deputy was partially fed by fear. "I'm okay."

He squeezed back.

She turned to watch the fire brigade attempt to save her house, but knew it was a lost cause. The few things she'd brought with her from Los Angeles, her mother's paintings, her mother's diary, which she'd tucked into the nightstand next to the bed…she'd probably lose them all.

But she was safe, she reminded herself. At least for now.

THE KILLER WAS growing desperate. Karine had escaped every single trap he'd laid.

She was smarter than her mother. Much smarter than the killer had given her credit for, it seemed.

But self-preservation was a strong motivation. He couldn't make it in prison.

The plan was risky, but he didn't see any other way. A more hands-on approach was needed.

Face to face. Direct.

It was time to put an end to Karine Eloi's meddling.

Chapter Twenty-Three

The EMT insisted on taking her to the hospital to be treated for smoke inhalation. Omar held her hand the entire way and only left her side when the doctor demanded he do so. Deputy Coben stopped by to take their statements and relay that the fire had been put out at her house. The second floor had come through relatively unscathed, but the main floor had suffered extensive damage. A city engineer would have to sign off on the building's structural integrity and the house would require thousands of dollars of renovation before she could move back in. And, in an uncharacteristically kind move, Deputy Coben had brought her a change of clothing, Crocs, her purse, and her phone, both a bit waterlogged, but because they'd been in her second-floor bedroom, still usable.

After hours of oxygen, blood tests and waiting around, she was finally discharged at half past midnight with instructions to take it easy for a couple of days.

James West was waiting for her and Omar outside the hospital in a sleek black four-door.

"I called him for a ride," Omar said. Her arm was tucked through his as he led her to the car.

"That was a good idea," she said, the cool night air singeing her lungs. "He can drop you off at your place and then I can ride with him to the B and B. I'll need to take a room there until I can figure out what to do with the house."

Omar stopped walking. "You'll stay with me."

She peered up at him. "I can't ask you to put me up. Not when things between us are so—"

"Karine, things will never be so bad between us that I won't be there for you when you need me."

The feeling behind his words struck her so forcefully, especially after the last twenty-four hours they'd spent together, that her knees threatened to buckle.

Omar caught her around the waist. "Are sure you're okay? Maybe we should have the doctor check you out one more time."

"No, no, I'm fine. Just tired."

The expression on his face said he wasn't convinced, but he guided her the rest of the way to the car.

James drove them back to Omar's house. Karine did her best to avoid looking over at the charred remains of her childhood home, but she couldn't help stealing a few glances. It looked like Deputy Coben had downplayed the damage to the house. It would take a lot of time, work and money to renovate. She'd seen the name of the homeowner's insurance company in the papers her lawyer had sent her when he'd transferred the title to her name. She'd look into all that later. Right now, she just wanted to sleep.

James left Omar to fuss over her, and he did an admirable job. The nightgown she'd been wearing was a lost cause, but Omar loaned her a T-shirt and, after assuring him at least a half dozen times that she was fine, had finally left her alone in his guest room.

As tired as her body was, she could only seem to sleep in snatches of time. Her dreams were a slideshow replay of the night she'd spent making love with Omar under the stars, the hurt she'd seen reflected in his eyes when she'd told him she couldn't be more than his friend, and the fear she'd felt when she'd thought the fire and smoke in her house might overtake her. Her father's words rang over and over in her head, accompanying the montage.

If you ever fall in love, and I hope you do, you'll see how hard it is to walk away.

She awoke, tangled in the sheets, her breath coming fast, burning her healing lungs. She reached for the glass of water Omar had left for her on the night table.

Even after everything they'd been through, he was by her side, taking care of her. She was terrified of moving her relationship with Omar from friendship into romance, but what if she was on the cusp of losing something even more precious? Because almost being burned to a crisp had made one thing crystal-clear.

She loved Omar.

And not as just a friend.

She'd loved him for a long time now, years in fact, but she'd been too much of a coward to do anything about it.

You'll see how hard it is to walk away.

Just the thought of walking away brought on an excruciating pain.

She swung her feet to the floor and stood, buoyed by the need to tell Omar how she felt. To fix what she'd broken.

He'd poured his heart out to her, and she'd said no.

The memory ripped a low groan out of her.

She had to make things right between them.

She shot a glance at the bedside clock: 5:05 a.m. Omar was an early riser, but five in the morning was probably pushing it.

She padded from the room and down the hall, each creak of his refinished hardwood floors sounding like the blast from a bullhorn to her ears.

Omar's door was slightly open, but she couldn't see the bed from the hall. No sound came from inside his room though.

He was still asleep, which made sense after the night they'd had. It had taken her years to get to the point where she was ready to admit to him and herself that she loved him. She could wait a few more hours.

She turned back toward the guest room, the floor creaking underneath her feet again.

"I can see your shadow. I know you're out there. Hovering. Are you going to come in or not?" Omar called from inside the room.

She pushed the door open.

He sat up in the bed, bare-chested, his reading glasses on and his phone in his hand.

"I didn't want to wake you," she said, suddenly shy.

"I've been awake for a while now. How are you feeling?"

"Fine." The word came out as a croak. She cleared her throat. "I'm fine. Fine."

He gave her a wry smile. "I'm glad to hear you're fine, fine. Are you hungry? I can make us some breakfast." He set his phone on the bedside table and placed his glasses next to them.

"No, I'm not hungry," she said, stepping into the room as he swung his feet to the floor, preparing to stand.

"Okay." He shot her another curious look. "Do you need something? Is there something I can get for you?"

"I love you." The words burst out of her, unwilling to be contained any longer.

Her declaration appeared to have shocked Omar into silence.

She took advantage of his temporary speechlessness and continued. "I love you and I was afraid. You have been the one constant in my life. The one person who was always there. Who understood me. My best friend. And I was afraid of that changing. But then there was the fire, and my father said something about how hard it is to walk away from someone you love, and he was right." She was babbling, she knew it, but she didn't seem to be able to stop herself.

"Ever since you drove away from me yesterday, I haven't been able to stop imagining my life without you in it, and it was more terrifying than being in that fire because I knew that you would move heaven and earth to get me to safety if you could, but if you weren't even there? If you weren't even in my life anymore? That, I couldn't stand. And then I realized that the reason I couldn't stand it was because I love you. I've loved you for a really long time, to be honest. So long, I don't even know when it started. Maybe forever." She took a breath. The deluge of words had given her healing lungs a bit of a workout, but she did want to end on a positive note. "So, yeah, I love you."

Silence seemed to hang between them for an interminable amount of time before Omar spoke. "So you're not afraid anymore."

"I'm terrified. But I'm more afraid I'd lose you, and I think that's what would happen if I didn't tell you how I feel."

Omar sighed and the faint smile that had been turning up the edges of his mouth died. "Karine, I don't want you to say anything because you think you'll lose me."

"No, that's not why…" She crossed the room and sat next to him on the bed. "I'm messing this up completely. I love you. I am more sure about that than I have been about anything in my life ever. It was always easier to pretend my feelings were just platonic because you were here and I was in Los Angeles. But now, I don't want to pretend anymore. I don't even think I could after the other night."

The sexy grin slid back onto Omar's face. "I was that good, huh?"

She slapped his chest and rolled her eyes. "I'm pouring my heart out here."

He grabbed the hand she'd hit him with. "Yes. I'm sorry. Continue," he said with faux seriousness.

"I love you and I don't want to go back to just being friends." And there was nothing faux about how serious she was.

Omar leaned forward, kissing her softly.

She tried deepening the kiss, but he pulled back. "I want nothing more than to ravish you right now, but the doctor said you need to take it easy."

She eyed his sculpted abdominals. "What I have in mind can be very relaxing."

Omar laughed, but shook his head. He scooted back on the bed, taking her with him. "Neither one of us got a lot of sleep last night. I think I'd like to just lie here and hold you." He lay down, making room for her to stretch out next to him. He wrapped his arm around her, pulling her in close.

She hooked her leg over his, her hand caressing his chest. “How long do you think we can stay like this?”

He dropped a kiss on the top of her head. “I was thinking forever. What do you think?”

“Sounds good to me.”

Chapter Twenty-Four

Omar's side of the bed was still warm when she awoke later that morning, but he was gone. In his place was a note.

Results on the water and soil samples came in. Didn't want to wake you. Back soon.

Karine was annoyed that he'd gone to see his friend without her.

She dressed, considering whether she should give Omar a call and meet up with him and his colleague, but decided against it. This was part of his job, and she was sure he would bring her up to speed the moment he got back. And she could read him the riot act for leaving her out of the loop then.

She slipped her sockless feet into Crocs and headed downstairs.

Karine filled the electric teakettle, then turned to see what she could find in the fridge for breakfast, and yelped.

A face stared at her through the windowpane in the back door. It took a moment for her brain to catch up with her vision and put two and two together.

"Daton?" She put the kettle on the warming plate and

switched it on before marching to the door. "Daton, you just about gave me a heart attack. What are you doing?"

Daton raised both hands in the air, an embarrassed blush flushing his cheeks. "I'm sorry. I didn't mean to scare you. I rang the doorbell. No one answered, but your car was at your house and… I guess I got worried. I heard about the fire at your place and with everything that's been going on and the situations you've found yourself in lately, I just wanted to make sure everything was okay."

Her heart was still beating furiously, but she felt her mouth turn up in the beginning of a smile. "The situations I've found myself in, huh? I guess I can't argue that I have gotten into a bit of trouble lately. Come in." She stepped aside to let him enter. "I was just about to have some tea. Or I could make you some coffee. Would you like to join me?"

"I would love tea." He beamed.

The water for their tea was already beginning to boil. She reached into the cabinet over the sink and drew out two mugs and two tea bags.

"I am sorry I startled you. How are you doing?"

Karine carried the mugs and tea bags to the kettle. "I'm fine. Frustrated. I guess I might have expected too much when I came to town. Finding new information about a twenty-three-year-old murder… I knew it wouldn't be easy, but I didn't realize just how hard it was going to be." She poured the boiling water into the mugs and passed one to Daton. "Sugar." She pointed to the bowl next to the kettle and pulled two spoons from the drawer to her left, handing one to him. She used the other to shovel two generous spoonsful of sugar in her cup. She took a sip and let the hot, soothing scent and taste of the chamomile engulf her.

Daton dipped the spoon into the bowl and sprinkled half a teaspoon of sugar into his cup. "Could I trouble you for a little milk?"

"Sure." She turned her back to him and went to the fridge.

"I have to confess, I'm kind of relieved your investigation hasn't been as fruitful as you'd hoped," he said.

"Why?" She grabbed the milk and turned to him with a frown.

"Because whoever killed Marilee is out there and you asking questions is clearly putting them on edge. I think you should consider leaving the investigating to the proper authorities."

Karine slid the milk across the counter, her frown deepening. "You're not the first person to suggest that." She took another sip of her tea. "But it feels like the answer is right there in front of me. I just can't fit all the pieces of the story together in a way that makes sense."

"The pieces of the story?" Daton wrapped his hands around his mug.

Karine took another long drink from her mug before she answered. "That's how I think about it. Like the story behind what led to my mom's death. There's the love letter I found, and mom's intervention into the situation between Principal Howser and Meghan. And, of course, the email from Amber that started this whole thing." She yawned, a sudden desire for a nap overwhelming her. She felt loose. Not so much tired, but like she wouldn't mind a quick nap. She shook her head to clear her mind. "I can't help but feel that if I just knew what Amber was going to tell me, I'd have the answer I needed."

"Yes, I'm sure you would," he said carefully.

A warning prickled at the back of her neck. "This tea seems to really be taking effect. Let's move into the living room where we can be more comfortable and, if I fall asleep while we're talking, you can just leave me on the sofa," she joked.

Daton didn't smile, but he did follow her into the living room.

She didn't make it to the sofa though. The curtains on Omar's large picture window were open to the street. The driveway was empty, as was the space on the street in front of the house.

"Daton, where is your car?" she asked, leaning against the window as much to hold herself upright as to get a good look up and down the street. No black Porsche in sight.

"I parked on a service road about a quarter mile from here. And I didn't drive the Porsche. It's too conspicuous."

The warning tingle turned into a warning torrent. Karine looked at Daton. Two Datons actually. Her vision swam. "What did you do to me?"

"Just a sedative. Oops." Daton reached out, grabbing her teacup before she dropped it with one hand and her arm with the other. He led Karine to the sofa. "You should sit before you fall down."

"You drugged me."

The two Datons sat next to her on the sofa. "Yes. It will be easier this way."

"Easier." She blinked and he came into focus. She fought to make sense of what was happening, but her mind seemed to be moving too slowly. "Why?"

He sighed, a sad smile playing over his lips. "Because you are too much like your mother."

"My mother?" His words weren't making any sense.

"Yes, your mother. I didn't want to kill her, either, but she wouldn't just mind her business. Well, you've seen how she was. Sticking her nose in Principal Howser's business and everyone else's around town. She was just so self-righteous. So sure she was always right. There was never any gray area with her, just black and white. Well, life isn't just black and white. There's a lot of gray. I tried to make her understand, but she just wouldn't."

Karine had to fight to hold her head up. She couldn't believe what she was hearing. The man she'd thought was her mother's friend had killed her. "You killed my mother."

"Yes, I did." He nodded solemnly. "You should understand that I didn't want to, or even mean to. I went to the house to try to talk some sense into her. To appeal to her as a friend. But, like I said, self-righteous. I lost my temper. It was an accident, but if I'd called the police and said that, then everything else would come out."

"What…out?" She wanted to hear the whole story. She deserved answers, but she wasn't sure she could remain conscious for much longer.

"The dumping."

Her head fell to the side, which Daton must have taken as a sign of her surprise.

"Yeah, the dumping your boyfriend is looking into. Spindler Plastics has been burying waste in the Carling Lake Forest on and off for years. Decades, actually. Not all the time, but it was a good way to cut back on expenses during a hard period. Your mother was always in those damned woods. She saw something she shouldn't have. I'd just taken over the company less than a year earlier and she figured I must not know about it. She came to me because she thought I'd take care of it. She believed in me." He sounded wistful. "It never occurred to her that I knew about it. I'd authorized it."

"Why?" Just getting the one word out had felt like a Herculean task. She was fading fast with no idea what Daton planned for her once she was unconscious or how she'd get out of it.

Omar. If she could just get to her phone. He'd said he'd be back soon. How long had he been gone?

"Because my father was a terrible businessman and my mother spent money like we were printing it in the basement. The company was going to go under, and then we'd have nothing. Everything my grandfather had worked for, the family name, everything I'd planned for my own future would have been gone. I couldn't let that happen. I tried to explain that to your mother."

"What…do…with me?"

Daton trailed a finger down her cheek.

She shuddered at his touch.

"If I thought I could convince you to keep quiet, I would, but like I said, you're just too much like your mother. Too tenacious. Too determined. I tried, I really did, to get you to walk away from this misguided investigation. A break-in. A fire. Nothing worked."

It was all coming together now.

"Amber."

Daton's lips twisted into a scowl. "Amber. Yes, I killed her too. She knew about the dumping. Had for years. It's hard to hide something as big as murder from someone you're living with. She put the pieces of your mother's murder together and came up with me. She didn't care."

Her heart cinched, and bile rose in her throat. All of the people who'd been closest to her mother had betrayed her.

"As long as the company made money, *I* made money, Amber didn't care," Daton continued. "But when I asked for a divorce, she used the video and the information about the dumping to get a very nice settlement out of me. And if she'd just left it at that, I wouldn't have been forced to deal with her. But what do they say about a woman scorned?" He nearly growled the words. "When I told her about Valerie's pregnancy, I could see it in her eyes. I mean, she already hated Valerie, but now she was giving me the child Amber and I couldn't create together. I think it tipped her into the deep end. Luckily, she was a loose-lipped drunk. She called me the night before she was going to meet with you. Taunting me about how she was going to tell you everything. It wasn't difficult to make her death look like an overdose. Too bad I can't do the same for you."

He picked up her mug and stood. "Don't worry. I'm going to clean up everything before we go. Can't leave any fingerprints. Hopefully, your disappearance will distract Omar from his investigation into the pollution in the forest. I'd hate to have to take care of him too. I don't think he'd be quite as easy to dispose of as you and Amber." Daton sighed heavily. "Oh well, no use in worrying about it. I'll cross that bridge if I get to it. Now, you just sit there and pass out. I'll only be a moment."

He strode into the kitchen.

Karine willed herself to find the strength and focus to

get up. The front door was only steps away. If she could just get outside, maybe one of the neighbors would see her and come over to help.

But the sedative was too strong. In the end, she did just what Daton had instructed her to do.

She passed out.

Chapter Twenty-Five

Omar met his friend Brett at a café midway between Carling Lake and Stunnersville, where Brett lived and worked. It was their usual place to meet whenever they carved out a few hours to catch up, although that had been happening far less frequently since Brett and his wife had had their first child.

Brett was already there when Omar arrived. He stood, and the two of them engaged in a quick bro hug before settling in. The waitress came by and took their drink and food order at the same time.

"Thanks for helping me out," Omar said once they'd placed their orders and the waitress had moved away from their table.

"Not a problem. I mean, you are paying for the tests, but I did put a rush on them for you." Brett grinned. "No charge."

Omar laughed. "Thanks. It pays to have friends in high places."

Brett's grin fell away as he reached for the file folder in the empty seat next to him. "I tested the soil, and it came back positive for high levels of methyl ethyl ketone or MEK."

"MEK." Omar frowned. "Karine was right then."

"Karine." Brett perked up. "Isn't that your best friend slash secret crush from Los Angeles?"

Omar rolled his eyes. He and Brett had been friends long enough that Brett had heard most of the Karine and Omar childhood stories, even though he and Karine had never met. Somewhere along the way, Brett had picked up on his feelings for Karine and he'd been gently teasing and alternatively pushing him to make a play for Karine ever since. Since he'd spent years telling Brett that he and Karine were just friends and that was all they'd ever be, he expected to take a bit of self-congratulatory ribbing when he told Brett that the relationship had moved out of the friend zone. Brett didn't disappoint.

"I knew it." Brett clapped. "It was written all over your face whenever you talked about the woman. You love her."

Omar held up a hand. "Whoa. Slow down. I mean, of course, I love her. She's my best friend and, yeah, okay, I have, and have had for some time, strong feelings for her. We're going to explore that, but I don't know," he said, letting his uncertainty hang out there for a moment. "She lives in Los Angeles. I live here. I don't know how we make a long distance relationship work."

"What are you talking about?" Brett said incredulously. "You've been making a long distance relationship work with Karine since I met you. But, look, if you don't want to do long distance, I don't blame you. But, my friend, take it from a happily married man. If this is the right woman for you, do whatever it takes to keep her. They hire park rangers in California, too, or so I hear."

The waitress returned with their food and they took a few minutes to eat.

Omar thought about what Brett had said. Could he really move to Los Angeles? He'd always imagined himself working until retirement in Carling Lake, but, really, there wasn't much keeping him in his hometown. Yes, he had many good friends, but his parents lived in Arizona now. Moving to California would actually put him closer to them than he was. And he did have an acquaintance who worked for the parks department in California. It had been a while since they'd spoken, but he could reach out to him, see what the employment layout around Los Angeles looked like.

Whoa. He slammed on his internal mental brakes. *Getting way ahead of yourself, Monroe. You and Karine literally just...*

Well, they'd literally just had an incredible night. And had agreed to see where a relationship went. Planning a move across the country might be just a bit too fast. But the seed had taken root. It felt fast, yes, but it also felt right.

He finished half his sandwich and requested a refill on his cola before he forced himself to focus on the task at hand.

"Tell me more about this MEK," he said, getting the conversation back on track. "I don't think I've ever heard of it."

"You might have heard it called butanone."

Omar shook his head. "Nope, never heard of it."

"It's a colorless chemical that only occurs in nature in small amounts."

"Yet the tests found high levels of this butanone in the soil samples I sent you."

Brett nodded. “Off-the-charts high. No way this is occurring naturally. Or by accident, in my expert opinion.”

That meant he’d been right all along. Someone was dumping the chemical in the Carling Lake Forest.

“Could this kill small animals?”

Brett tipped his head. “I did a little research after the results came in. I couldn’t find a study specifically looking at the effects of MEK on the environment, but acetone is a close chemical cousin to this stuff, and it definitely causes harm. In animals and in humans, if ingested in large enough quantities.”

“So it’s probably safe to say that this butanone is also dangerous. Certainly to smaller animals.”

“If I was in your place, I certainly wouldn’t dismiss the possibility. More testing would need to be done, but I’d say you found your pollutant.”

“So, I know what is poisoning my forest, but I still need to find out who is doing it and where the chemical is coming from.” Omar pushed his plate to the side and pulled out the map he’d taken down off the office bulletin board after John had ordered him to drop the investigation.

Brett had already inhaled his entire lunch, so he pushed his empty plate to the side as well.

Omar spread the map out between them. “Here are all the places where I found affected animals.” He pointed to the multiple red Xs that replaced the pins.

Brett studied the map for several minutes. “So we know the water isn’t affected. It’s just the soil.”

“Yes. Karine suggested that I test the soil because something hazardous might have seeped into it and the animals are affected when they burrow into the soil.”

"Or eat plants or insects that have absorbed the chemical." Brett looked thoughtful. "It's not a bad theory, but it's way out of my expertise."

Omar's, as well, but he did know someone who might be able to help. Karine wouldn't like asking her father for help though. He'd cross that bridge when he got there.

Brett leaned back in his chair. "So, what are you going to do now?"

"I don't know," Omar answered honestly. "My supervisor doesn't even want me on this. I have to have irrefutable proof of soil contamination before I take it to him."

Brett frowned. "Is this the same supervisor who supposedly sent the water samples to the state lab for testing?"

"Yes. Why do you say 'supposedly'?"

"That was the other thing I wanted to talk to you about and didn't want to put in an email or say over the phone. I called a friend of mine who still works at the state lab to confirm something on the water test results you sent me with the soil sample. My friend couldn't find any record of the lab having conducted the test on water sources in Carling Lake."

Omar sat stunned for a moment. "That can't be right. I sent you the test results."

Brett held his hands out. "All I can tell you is my friend says the test didn't come from the state lab."

The implication of the information hit him. "John falsified the report."

That meant there was a good possibility water sources could also be contaminated. And that John was aware of it. He knew about the contamination, knew who was causing it, and was probably taking a bribe to keep that information covered up.

Omar flagged down their waitress and asked for the check. He needed to get back to Carling Lake and figure out his next steps. He'd have to go over John's head, but he had no idea how far up the corruption went. He'd have to be careful.

His phone rang just as the waitress dropped the check off. He dug his phone and his wallet out of his pocket, answering the phone without looking at who was calling first.

"Hello?"

"Omar, it's James West."

Omar dropped enough cash to cover the bill and a generous tip on the table then stood. "James, can I call you back later? I've got a developing situation on my hands."

He said a hasty goodbye to Brett, who waved him off in understanding, then exited the restaurant.

"I don't think this can wait," James said. "The techs at West Investigations were able to clean up the video of the man skulking around Karine's house on the night of her mother's murder. They got a good shot of the intruder's face and I'm sending you a still shot of it now."

Omar put the phone on speaker and opened the new text message from James.

"Omar, Karine might need to brace herself—"

He should have heeded James's warning as well.

"Damn it," he said as the face in the photo registered in his brain.

The person creeping around the Eloi house on the night of Marilee's murder was none other than Marilee's close friend, Daton Spindler.

Chapter Twenty-Six

The first thing she became aware of was her throbbing head. The second was the fact that she was in a car. One was related to the other since her head was bouncing against something, not exactly hard, but not exactly softly either.

Karine tried to open her eyes, but they felt like they'd been glued closed. It took effort, but she finally forced them open.

She was definitely in a car. She raised her hands, surprised to find them bound together tightly with rope.

She turned her head slowly, her brain still thick with fog, but becoming clearer.

Daton.

His blurry figure was behind the steering wheel. He was taking her somewhere. Where? She couldn't remember. Had he told her?

He glanced across the car at her.

"You're awake." He didn't sound pleased.

Her mind was clearing slowly. Daton showing up at Omar's and drinking tea with her. Daton drugging her. Daton confessing to having killed her mother. And now he planned to kill her too.

Her limbs still felt like lead. She looked out of the window but could only see the road and trees. She didn't know where they were exactly, but it appeared to be remote.

Daton's phone was on the charger on the dashboard, but she doubted he'd let her make a call.

"Where are you taking me?"

Daton glanced at her again. "Someplace where no one will find you."

She pulled against the ropes. She had to get out of this car. She glanced around for a weapon, something, anything, to use to defend herself. She didn't see anything.

Bright lights flashed in the rearview mirror. A small compact car was barreling down on them. The driver honked, leaning on the horn.

Karine turned in the seat, her head throbbing. It was hard to see, but the driver…it was Richie Portman.

Richie honked again.

Daton looked in the rearview mirror. "What the…?"

"It's my neighbor. He must have seen you kidnapping me. I'm sure he's called the sheriff. You'll never get away with this. The only way out is to stop this now and turn yourself in."

"You think that's the only way?" Daton scoffed. "I've come too far to let a nosy neighbor get in my way."

He pulled a gun from between his seat and the console.

Karine shrank back, pressing herself to the door. "What are you doing with that?"

Daton didn't answer. He rolled his window down and reached his left arm out, holding the gun.

Pop. Pop.

There was no way the bullets could have hit Richie, not

with the angle Daton was holding the gun, but the shots had their desired effect.

Richie's car fell back a bit, but didn't stop following.

"Damn it," Daton snarled when he saw Richie still following. He stomped on the brakes.

The car skidded to a stop.

Richie swerved to avoid hitting them and sped past.

Daton hit the accelerator. He stuck his hand out the window again, and this time the bullets whizzed forward, slamming into the back of Richie's car.

Karine screamed. Richie was out there because of her. To help her. She couldn't let Daton hurt him.

Without thinking, she reached across the console and grabbed the steering wheel.

"Let go!" Daton yelled, trying to knock her hands away.

She fisted her hands and smacked him in the face.

"Damn." Daton brought a hand to his bloody nose, letting the gun fall into the footwell.

The car veered toward the trees at the side of the road. Karine grabbed the wheel, attempting to bring them back onto the asphalt. But Daton snatched the wheel, too, and he was stronger.

The front of the car dipped and then they were tumbling. Rolling over. Once. Twice. She thought a third time before the car stopped, upright.

"Ugh!" Her head felt like it had split in two.

Daton was unconscious, but she could see the rise and fall of his chest. He was alive.

Karine tried her door. It was jammed. But Daton's window was still open. It would mean crawling over him, but that seemed safer than staying in the car. As long as he didn't wake up.

She crawled over him, holding her breath and praying he'd remain unconscious until she was out. Richie had to have seen the wreck. If she could make it back to the road, they could drive to safety and send for help.

She was finally able to extricate herself.

"Karine!"

She looked up the incline. Richie stood at the side of the road, looking down.

"Karine. Hang on," he called again, sliding down the hill.

She started up, meeting him halfway.

Richie wrapped an arm around her and helped her the rest of the way. "I already called the sheriff," he said when they made it to the top.

She could hear the sirens, although they still sounded to be a ways off.

Richie glanced back down the incline at the wrecked car. "I guess I should call for an ambulance too." He loped off toward his car.

The sirens were getting louder, but it wasn't a sheriff's cruiser that turned the curve first.

Omar slammed his pickup into Park and jumped out, running to her. "Karine. Are you okay? Where is Daton?"

She pointed down the hill.

Omar glanced at the wreck then back to her. He cradled her face. "Are you sure you're okay? Did he hurt you?"

"No. I mean, I'm a little banged up and my head is killing me from the combination of the sedative and the accident, but no permanent damage."

A breath gushed out of Omar. He pulled her to his chest,

wrapping her in his arms. "Do you know how scared I was? When James called to say Daton was the man in the security video from your house and then Richie called the sheriff to say he'd seen Daton carrying you out through the woods behind my house. I thought—"

"I'm okay. I'm—oh!" Omar shifted her to the side. Threw her, really. "What?"

And then she saw.

Daton. On his knees at the edge of the road. He'd come to and crawled out of the car. And he had the gun.

Omar snatched his own weapon from its holster at his hip.

Karine screamed as the sound of gunshots exploded around them.

She crouched on the asphalt road, her hand covering her head.

"Karine, baby, it's over. It's over," Omar's soothing voice said next to her.

She raised her head. Daton lay in the grass beside the road. Completely still.

Omar helped her to her feet.

"It's over," he repeated.

This time, she believed him.

Epilogue

Karine stood on the street in front of her family home. Dealing with the arson inspector, the insurance company, and getting bids for repair and renovation had been grueling, especially since she'd had to do a lot of it long-distance. Omar had been an immense help there and, thankfully, the actual work that needed to be done to get the home in livable condition had begun a couple of weeks earlier. She planned to put her family home back together again and then put it on the market. It was time to move on.

Omar joined her in front of the house. He wrapped an arm around her shoulder and pulled her close to his side. "Are you doing okay?"

She looked up at him and smiled. "I'm better than okay."

And she was. The moment was tinged with sadness and nostalgia for what had been and what could have been under different circumstances. But mostly she felt hope and excitement.

She glanced at the house next door.

The For Sale sign in front of Omar's house now had a big red-and-white Sold sticker crisscrossing the Realtor's face. When she left Carling Lake in a few days, Omar would be leaving with her. He'd gotten a position with the California state park rangers and they were going to try to make a go of their relationship.

Daton had survived the gunshot injury to the shoulder and confessed to the attack on Karine on her first night in town, shooting at her and Omar in the parking lot of Barney's, killing his ex-wife, Amber, and bludgeoning Karine's mother to death. He'd also confessed to attacking Becky Portman after Shep had told him about the security video from the night of Marilee's murder. He'd had plans to make sure Richie also had a tragic accident, but events had spiraled beyond his control before he could get to it. Thankfully, his sister, Becky, had made a full recovery.

Daton and Spindler Plastics were facing a host of state and federal crimes arising from the environmental pollution Marilee had stumbled upon and ultimately lost her life because of. It turned out Daton was nowhere near the businessman his father and grandfather had been. Twenty-three years ago, the company had been headed toward dire financial straits when Daton came up with the idea of cutting costs by burying some of the chemical manufacturing waste deep in the Carling Lake woods. Unfortunately, Karine's mother had stumbled upon his men when they'd been engaged in the crime. She'd gone to her friend, believing he could not have been aware of what others in the company were doing and that he'd put a stop to it immediately and fix the issue. Once she realized that Daton had not only known about the pollution but condoned its illegal disposal, she'd decided to go to the authorities. Her mistake had been in telling her friend what she'd planned to do. Daton had tried everything he could think of to keep her from going to the police, but Marilee had loved Carling Lake too much to let anyone destroy it.

Daton said that on the night of her murder, he had only gone to try to talk Marilee into forgetting about what she'd seen, but that he'd lost his temper. He'd struck Marilee with the fireplace poker. He swore he hadn't meant to kill her and that he hadn't realized that Karine was home. The one good thing that had come out of her mother's death was that Daton had been so terrified that someone would discover what he'd done and why that he'd ceased the illegal dumping of waste. At least until six months ago when tough times had befallen the company once more and, feeling safe from ever being outed as Marilee's killer, he'd gone back to his illegal dumping scheme to save Spindler Plastics money.

Daton also hadn't known about the new, small, unobtrusive security cameras Marilee had installed in an attempt to catch her husband with his mistress. Nor had he known that she had confided in her friend Amber, who'd gotten the security recording and been stunned when she'd recognized the shadow creeping toward the Eloi house as her husband. She'd kept quiet for years, not even telling Daton about the video until he'd announced he'd wanted a divorce. Then she'd used it to extract a very generous settlement. But her conscience had begun weighing on her in the months before her death. She'd made a tragic mistake the night before her meeting with Karine in calling Daton after she'd been drinking and using pills. She'd let spill her plan to tell Karine what she knew and Daton had decided she had to go.

Deputy Shep Coben had known about the security cameras. He'd admitted to feeding Daton confidential information for years, not just about Marilee's case, though that was the initial reason Daton had made the alliance. Lance wanted to initiate formal disciplinary proceedings, but Shep had resigned and moved away from Carling Lake before he could be fired. Shep had bigger problems than losing his job, though. The prosecutor was planning to bring charges against him for misuse of public office, bribery and obstruction of justice, among other charges.

Karine knew in her gut that Shep at the very least must have suspected Daton of her mother's murder. She couldn't get it out of her head that maybe Shep hadn't missed the security camera at all. But her gut wasn't evidence, so it looked like Shep would get away with whatever crimes he might have committed.

John Huyton, Omar's supervisor, had also been let go for taking bribes from Daton and falsifying water testing reports. Word around town was that he had already made a deal with the state and federal prosecutors to testify against Daton.

Things between her and her father were still tense, but she'd told him everything she'd discovered about her mother's death, and Jean had vowed to be in court every day of Daton's trial. Her parents' marriage hadn't been perfect, but she'd seen how much her father had cared about her mother. And how much having people believe he could have been involved in her death had affected him. Omar was right. People made mistakes, and she wanted to have a relationship with her father.

She shook away the memories of the last several months and looked toward her future. She looked at Omar. "You ready?"

He leaned forward and pressed a kiss to her mouth. "Absolutely."

* * * * *

Look for more books in K.D. Richards's ongoing series, West Investigations, coming soon, only from Harlequin Intrigue!